NO ESCAPE

"I'm giving you warning now," Renda said, including all the convicts. "One move out of line and somebody shoots. You'll even think before spitting over the side of the wagon.

"You hesitate one second when you're told to do something, you're dead. You take one step in the wrong direction and you won't know what hit you." He turned to Bowen suddenly. "You understand that?"

Bowen nodded, looking up at Renda.

"Listen," Renda said, "I'll tell you something else. That stunt you pulled a while back...jumping off the wagon. You wouldn't get just twenty days for it the second time."

He looked over all the convicts. "You get past the guards, the Mimbres have got orders to take your scalp. You won't be brought back here...just part of you. To prove you're dead."

Bantam Books by Elmore Leonard
Ask your bookseller for the books you have missed

ESCAPE FROM FIVE SHADOWS

Elmore Leonard

BANTAM BOOKS

TORONTO · NEW YORK · LONDON · SYDNEY · AUCKLAND

ESCAPE FROM FIVE SHADOWS
A Bantam Book / published by arrangement with the author
Houghton Mifflin edition published May 1959
Bantam edition / August 1981
2nd printing . . . May 1985

ISBN 0-553-24863-4

Published simultaneously in the United States and Canada

Bantam Books are published by Bantam Books, Inc. Its trade-
mark, consisting of the words "Bantam Books" and the por-
trayal of a rooster, is Registered in U.S. Patent and Trademark
Office and in other countries. Marca Registrada. Bantam
Books, Inc., 666 Fifth Avenue, New York, New York 10103.

PRINTED IN THE UNITED STATES OF AMERICA

O   11 10 9 8 7 6 5 4

ESCAPE
FROM FIVE
SHADOWS

ONE

Karla hesitated in the doorway of the adobe, then pushed open the screen door and came out into the sunlight as she heard again the faint, faraway sound of the wagon; and now she looked off toward the stand of willows that formed a windbreak along the north side of the yard, her eyes half closed in the sun glare and not moving from the motionless line of trees.

She waited for the wagon to appear—a girl not yet twenty, with clear dark eyes, a clean-lined delicately featured face that was brown from the sun, and black hair that suggested Spanish-Indian blood, though her hair was cut short, almost boyishly short, and brushed back from her temples; a girl wearing a man's blue chambray shirt tucked into a gray skirt that fell almost to her rope-soled sandals.

Now she could hear the horses splashing over the creek that passed through the willows. The team and wagon appeared but the girl waited until the two riders who trailed the wagon came into view before she turned to the adobe.

"They're coming now."

Her father, John Demery, appeared in the doorway thumbing a suspender strap over his shoulder, up over long-sleeved woolen underwear. And now his face creased to an expression of almost pain as he looked off into the yellow-white sun glare. The willow trees added color to the scene and beyond them, towering, sloping out of the distance, the foothills of the Pinaleño Mountains were striped with the black shadow lines of barrancas and pine stands; but here on the flat land, looking straight out from the adobe east, then sweeping south, there was an unvarying sameness of mesquite and sun glare and the thin faint line of distant mountains was part of another world.

Demery's long adobe, his corral and outbuildings, were here of necessity. On the Hatch & Hodges Stage Line map his place was indicated at Station #3 on the Central Mail run. Locally, it was the Pinaleño station—thirteen miles southeast of Fuegos, the nearest town; and six miles also south of the convict camp at Five Shadows.

1

The wagon now approaching the station was from the convict camp. Karla was certain of this from the moment she'd heard the first faint creaking sound from the willows. She kept her eyes on the wagon, watching the driver gradually turning the team to come in broadside to the adobe.

Now one of the riders, a shotgun across his pommel, spurred to swing in on the near side. As he did, Karla said, "Mr. Renda himself."

Demery half turned from the door. "I'll get the voucher. The sooner they're out of here the better." But he hesitated, looking out toward the wagon again. "Is your friend along?"

"I don't know," Karla answered, not looking around, her gaze still going out across the yard. "He could be one of those two in back. But I can't see their faces yet."

"Or their numbers," Demery said. He turned back into the dimness of the adobe.

Frank Renda, with the shotgun, was coming directly toward her; but the second rider crossed the yard diagonally and remained on the far side of the wagon. He carried a Winchester straight up, the stock resting on his thigh and his hand gripping it through the lever.

The two men whom Karla could not yet see, who sat in the back of the empty wagon with their legs hanging over the end gate, and the driver, looked toward the adobe as they drew nearer. They wore curl-brimmed, preshaped straw hats. Their shirts and Levis were faded and sweat-stained and a number was stenciled on the right thigh of each of the three men's Levis. The same number was stenciled in back, below the beltline. The driver wore number 22; the men on the end gate, 17 and 18.

Frank Renda dismounted. He let his reins trail and came toward Karla carrying the shotgun under his arm—a man about her father's age, in his mid-forties, but heavier than her father, thicker through chest and shoulders, and wearing a mustache, a full, untrimmed tobacco-stained mustache that almost completely covered the firm line of his mouth.

He stopped in front of Karla, blocking her view of the men in the wagon. He stood close to her, the shotgun barrel touching her skirt, but she didn't move, not even eyes, and she returned his gaze.

2

"Where's my stuff, Karla?" He smiled saying this, but the smile was not in the sound of his voice.

"In the shed," Karla answered.

Renda motioned toward the open shed that extended out from the east wall of the adobe. Karla saw the rider who was still mounted walk his horse toward it, his Winchester across his pommel now. Then, as the wagon moved on, passing close to her, she glanced at the two convicts on the end gate.

For a moment her eyes held on the man wearing number 18. She looked away then, quickly, her gaze going to the shed: feeling an unexpected excitement in seeing him and suddenly afraid it would show on her face.

She did not try to explain the feeling, for it was not something that could be reasonably explained, even to herself. This was the ninth time she had seen him. She was sure of that. Eight times in the past month, delivering mail to the convict camp, she had taken the trail down through the canyon and passed him on the new road. Riding along the stretch of road construction, passing the convicts and the guards, then seeing him, watching him until it would be obvious that she was watching and then she would look away.

Eight times this way and always with the feeling that she knew what he was thinking, knowing that he was watching the guards, following their moves and trying to locate the ten or twelve Apache trackers who were always mounted and always somewhere above the canyon but seldom in sight.

Each time she had wanted to say to him, "Please don't try it. Please." Again for a reason she did not even attempt to understand, though she wondered if others sensed his wanting to escape as strongly as she did.

That was part of it: the knowing what he was thinking. That and the feeling that she had known him a long time; as if he were a boy she had gone to school with in Willcox and had been close to and had seen every day and was now ~eeing again after a lapse of six or seven years. But, she ~~ever laid eyes on him before a month ago and even ~ did not know his name. This was the first ~ been brought to Pinaleño with the supply

~ hed Renda walking off after the wagon,

3

seeing, beyond him, the wagon pulling up in front of the open shed.

She could feel the rider with the Winchester looking at her, but she did not raise her eyes to him. Her father had said that his name was Brazil—Renda's head guard. And her father had said he was a gunman; a man paid purely and simply for his gun and probably deserved to be wearing a straw hat and numbered pants as much as any convict in the camp.

The driver was standing in the wagon bed now, his head even with the shed roof. He would stoop under it, into the straight-line shade of it to take the sacks of flour and dried beans and salt that the two men who had been on the end gate handed up to him. He would drag the sacks to the front of the wagon and stack them, taking his time, as if trying to make this last as long as possible. Now and again he would glance at Karla.

She noticed this, but most of the time her eyes remained on the convict wearing number 18.

His sleeves were cut off at the shoulders and she had never seen a man's arms burned such a deep brown. Black copper, she thought. And in the shadow of his hatbrim his face seemed even darker. It went through the girl's mind that with shoulder-length hair and features that were coarse he could pass for a San Carlos Apache. Still, even though she had never seen him without the straw hat, she knew his hair was sand colored, just as she knew his eyes would be blue.

At this moment she knew he was watching Renda and the one called Brazil. Not looking at them directly, but watching every move they made from the shadow of the curled hatbrim.

Karla half turned as the screen door opened. "He's here," she said, a trace of excitement in the tone of her voice.

Her father stepped out into the yard. He carried a Voucher for Supplies and Services Rendered, made out by Seely, Lewis & Foss, Government Contractors. As he looked toward the wagon he asked, "Which one?"

"He's wearing 18."

"I can't make out figures from here."

"The one without sleeves in his shirt."

Demery squinted in the sunlight, study̶ "He looks like any other jailbird to me."

4

"You have to see him up close," Karla said.

"Why do you think he's any different from the rest?"

"I don't know ... haven't you ever had a feeling about a person?" She glanced at her father. "Like Ma ... you liked her right away, didn't you? You didn't ask to see her papers before you married her."

"You're planning to marry him, are you?"

"I'm drawing a parallel."

"Sis, the difference is I didn't meet your mother in a convict camp."

"How do you know why he's there?" Karla said hotly. "For all we know he was hungry and killed somebody else's cow. You can't blame a man for something like that."

Demery nodded. "Only maybe it wasn't a cow," he said mildly, glancing at Karla. "A nice-looking boy who doesn't look like he should be in convict clothes, so you feel sorry for him."

"It's more than that," Karla said earnestly. "But I can't explain it."

"Like getting a warm feeling for a boy at school."

"You make it sound ridiculous."

"Sis, that's what I'm trying to do. You don't even know his name."

Karla looked at her father hopefully. "I was going to ask you to ask Mr. Renda."

"What good would it do you to know it?"

"I was thinking of writing to Mr. Martz," Karla said. "He's in the courthouse every day. He could look up his record—"

"You'd write all the way to Prescott to find out why he's in?"

"I can't think of any other way."

"Waste Lyall Martz's valuable time on an errand like that—"

"He'd do it for me."

"Sis, you're sure of yourself. I'll say that."

"Don't you think he would?"

"I'm not going to encourage you."

Karla hesitated. "Will you ask Mr. Renda his name?"

Demery shook his head. "You might have a pure, kindly feeling about the boy, but don't ask me to be a party to it."

"Then you won't."

"Ask him yourself."

"He'd think it was funny. A girl asking."

"No funnier than me doing it. 'Frank, what's that boy's name, number 18? Karla's got a warm feeling for him, wants to know all about him.'"

Karla grinned. "Not like that. Just say you think you recognize him from somewhere. Or he looks like someone who used to work for you. I couldn't tell Mr. Renda that, but you could."

"With Frank's shifty-eyed nature," Demery said, "right away he'd suspect something."

Karla winked at him. "Not the way you'd handle it, Pa. Smooth as silk."

Demery eyed his daughter in silence. "You know where you ought to be? Up in Prescott with Lyall. He'd use you to soften up the juries."

Karla smiled. "You'll ask him?"

Demery looked off toward Renda who stood near the wagon watching the supplies being loaded. He called out, "Frank—" and as Renda turned, "Here's your voucher!"

Renda left the wagon and as he reached them he said to Demery, "Don't strain yourself."

Demery moved to the door. He held the screen open for Renda, saying, "You generally sign the voucher on the bar, don't you? Why take extra steps?" Renda said nothing. He walked past Demery into the adobe. Demery followed him, turning to wink at Karla before the screen closed behind him.

Karla walked toward the shed now. As she reached the corner of the adobe, Brazil, still mounted, called, "Don't get too close . . . one of them's liable to grab you." He grinned at her, cradling the Winchester in the crook of his arm and took out tobacco to make a cigarette.

The man in the wagon bed, a tall, gaunt-faced dark-bearded convict, his hands on his hips, looked down at her. "That wouldn't be so bad, would it?"

Karla said nothing. She looked away indifferently, but gradually her eyes returned to the convict wearing number 18.

He lifted a bundle of pick handles over the sideboard, then leaned against a support post, removing his hat. As Karla watched, she saw it: his hair light brown though it appeared darker, wet with perspiration. His features were even, features that were almost soft, yet di̶s̶t̶i̶n̶c̶t̶i̶v̶e̶ would be easily remembered. Part of his forehead was a white band that the sun had not reached and it contrasted vividly with the deep tan of his jaw line.

Karla turned, hearing the screen door again. Renda was saying something as they approached. Then, as they drew nearer, she heard her father say, "They got here about suppertime yesterday."

"If I'd known," Renda said, "I could've picked them up last night."

"Do you think," Demery asked, "I should have ridden all the way up to tell you?"

"You could've sent Karla."

"Look," Demery stated. "You pay five dollars more freight costs and it's delivered right to your door."

Renda shook his head. "Willis figured this way was cheaper."

"Was he sober when he figured it?"

Renda smiled now. "That's no way to talk about our superintendent. Willis Falvey knows his figures."

Karla asked, "And how does Mrs. Falvey like living at a convict camp?"

"Lizann?" Renda said with mock surprise. "Why Lizann likes it up there fine." He would have said more, but Brazil called out to him—

"Frank! I'm sitting in the sun while you pass the time of day!"

"There's a man that's all business," Renda said. He motioned the two convicts onto the wagon, then called to Brazil, "Let's go!" He walked past Demery and Karla and mounted his chestnut mare. From the saddle he said, "Karla, we'll visit awhile the next time you bring the mail."

He reined the mare and rode straight out from the adobe to meet the wagon making a wide, slow turn to head back toward the willows.

For a moment Karla and her father watched the wagon in silence. Finally Karla said, "Did you ask him?"

Demery nodded, still watching the wagon as it drew near the willows. "I asked him."

"What did he say?"

"Enough so you won't have to write Lyall." Demery looked at his daughter then. "A year ago he was convicted of cattle rustling and tried at Prescott. He's already spent nine months in Yuma. He's been here three months and he's got

7

six years to go of a seven-year sentence. That, Sis, is the nice-looking boy you have the warm feeling for."

For a moment Karla said nothing. Then, "And his name?"

"Corey Bowen," her father answered.

TWO

THE DRIVER, Earl Manring, drew in on the reins as the wagon reached the willow trees that lined the creek bank. He stood up, kneeling one knee on the seat, and looked back at Renda. "We better water first. Right?"

Renda neck-reined his mare closer to the wagon. "All right." He looked at Bowen and Ike Pryde sitting on the end gate. "Get a drink," he told them, then rode over to the willow shade where Brazil was dismounting.

Brazil drank first, then Renda; and now, as they watered their horses, both of them watched the three men kneeling at the creek a few feet from the wagon team.

Manring cupped the water in his hands and raised it to his mouth. He drank the water, but his hands remained at his face and he said to Bowen, "There'll be a better time than today. Today's not right for it."

Bowen said nothing. He was lying on his stomach now with his elbows propped under him, staring at the sandy creek bed.

"If I know it," Manring said, "then Renda knows it."

Not looking at him, Bowen said, "You don't know anything."

"Listen. It's written on you like a sign. You don't talk and you keep watching Renda...thinking he don't know it."

Ike Pryde, the convict wearing number 17, half turned. He was in his late thirties, older than Bowen and Manring by not more than ten years; though he looked old enough to be their father. He had taken off his hat and in the sunlight his skull showed white through his thin, close-cropped hair. His face was hard-lined and rarely changed its expression; but age showed in his eyes and in the stoop-shouldered way he moved. Six years at Yuma before the road gang. Six years that had added sixteen to his life. His eyes raised to Earl Manring as he turned.

"Leave him alone," he muttered.

"If he'd think for a minute," Manring said, "he'd change his mind."

9

Bowen leaned closer to the bank to scoop water. "I'll say it once more. You don't know anything."

"I know somewhere between here and camp you're going into the woods."

"You think what you want," Bowen said.

Manring's jaw was clenched. "This isn't the way to do it! You got no horse. You got *nothing!*"

"Earl"—Pryde's lips barely moved—"you're going to get your jaw broke."

Renda and Brazil came out of the willow shade. Bowen rose and moved to the end of the wagon, then looked forward to the team again as he saw Pryde staring in that direction. Manring stood by one of the horses adjusting the harness and Renda was leaning over his saddle horn, saying something to him.

They forded the creek. On the other side, they followed wagon tracks that formed a long, slow-sweeping curve up to the jackpines along the crest, then skirted the shoulder of the hill before sloping down again and after this the trail kept to deep, rock-rimmed draws that twisted through the hills.

Renda rode in the lead now, turning in his saddle every few minutes to look back at the wagon. Behind the supply load, he could not see the two men on the end gate. They were Brazil's concern. Brazil and his Winchester brought up the rear, keeping not more than twenty feet behind the wagon.

The two men on the end gate had not spoken since leaving the creek. Now, unexpectedly, Pryde said, "In another mile we reach the steep part."

They sat with their legs hanging, their shoulders hunched forward and their eyes on the trail falling away beneath their feet.

Bowen said nothing.

"It's steep enough," Pryde mumbled, "that we'll have to get off and lean on a wheel."

"I know that," Bowen said.

"How? This is your first trip."

"I was told."

"What else were you told?"

"That was enough."

Pryde's eyes raised momentarily to Brazil following them. "That boy's dying to use his Winchester."

"If you want to talk," Bowen said, "tell me something I don't know."

Pryde's jaw tightened, then relaxed slowly. "You're tough, huh?"

Bowen didn't answer.

"It takes more than being tough," Pryde said. He was silent for a moment. "You're thinking when we reach the grade and have to get off, that's the time to go. Then or never." Pryde paused again. "I'll tell you one time. Don't do it today."

Bowen said, "You and Manring."

"Manring has his own reason. I don't know what that was, but I'm telling you what I feel."

"You didn't say anything at the creek."

"It wasn't the same then. If you wanted to jump, that was your business. Now there's something wrong. That man with the Winchester knows what's about."

Bowen's eyes raised. "He looks the same as always."

"You don't *see* a difference," Pryde growled. "You *feel* it."

"Well, I don't *feel* it."

"You haven't been locked up long enough."

"I'd say long enough," Bowen answered.

Pryde waited. "After six years you know things. Things you didn't know before. I don't know how, but you do."

Bowen glanced up, then looked down at the wagon ruts again. "When you were at Yuma...did you ever try to run?"

"Twice."

"How long before they caught you?"

"A day one time. Four the next. They paid the Pimas fifty dollars to bring you back."

"When you broke out...did it *feel* like it was the right time?"

Pryde hesitated. "I don't remember."

"But you're telling me one time's wrong and another time isn't."

Pryde said, "Go to hell then." But he added, "Even if you get clear, Renda's got better than Pimas. You know that."

"So it's a chance all the way."

"You don't outrun the trackers he's got. They been reading sign since they were little kids."

"That's not something to worry about now."

"But that Winchester is," Pryde said.

The trail began to rise again. Bowen could feel the wagon slanting upward and his hand gripped the end gate chain close to his right leg to steady himself.

Another twenty minutes, Bowen thought. He pictured the ride in earlier that morning, coming down the steep grade and studying the country carefully as they did, then reaching this section that clung to the hill shoulder and dropped off steeply on the right side.

No, he thought, may be only ten minutes to the grade. But it doesn't make any difference how long. When you reach it, they'll pull you off the wagon and you'll know.

He thought of what Pryde had told him about them being ready and expecting him to break.

That was foolishness. You don't *feel* things. Even if you do, you don't bet on a feeling. You don't stake something big on it.

They're always ready, he thought. It's just a question of moving when they're *least* ready.

A convict on the road gang named Chick Miller had described the trail between the camp and Pinaleño. Every foot of it that he could remember. He had told Bowen, "Going there isn't the time. But when you're coming back, Renda rides in front. If he was to stay behind, then the load would be between him and the driver and some places the trail is only as wide as the wagon. That means only one man's in back to watch you. Now I'd say a man's best time would be when you reach the high grade and have to get off. Now you're on the ground, getting the feel of it under your shoes ... and your rear guard is worrying whether the wagon's going to come sliding back at him."

He remembered Chick winking and saying, "That's the time, Corey. Right then."

And when he asked Chick why he had never tried it, the answer was that he was along in years and his legs wouldn't bear up under the running. "Boy ... you'll run till they drop off."

Bowen had waited, every day thinking about it, picturing himself doing it ... and finally this morning he was picked for the Pinaleño trip and the time had come.

Maybe Chick told Manring, Bowen thought. That's how he knows. And Pryde picked it up from Manring.

His eyes raised to Brazil again. The Winchester was

across his lap. Of course they're ready, he thought again; but you catch them when they're least—

Suddenly he saw his error.

Why should they be least ready at the grade? Because Chick said so?

If Brazil thought you had even a halfway better chance there he'd be readier than he was ever ready!

Why is being on the ground an advantage? Your back's to him then!

He breathed in and out slowly and thought, more calmly: You're facing him now. You're looking right at him and you even know when he scratches himself.

He glanced over the side of the wagon. The trail dropped off abruptly, slanting steeply for twenty-five or thirty feet. Then thick brush. Brush and scrub pine and rock and beyond that a second slope that was more gradual.

But how do you make the Winchester wait five seconds?

He noticed loose stones along the edge of the trail and he thought: One of those could stop him long enough.

But how do you know there'll be one where you jump off? We could come to a bare stretch just as—

He stopped . . . his eyes on Brazil. He watched Brazil raise the rifle barrel and rest it in the crook of his left arm. His right hand came up and across his chest and two fingers hooked into the shirt pocket to bring out the tobacco sack.

You're looking at it, Bowen thought, knowing it, being sure of it, and feeling the excitement inside of him now and trying not to show it.

You don't sit and think about it. You go or you don't go.

The crook of Brazil's left arm squeezed the barrel tightly as he poured tobacco into the troughed square of cigarette paper. Both of his hands were busy; both of them away from the trigger of the Winchester.

You go!

It was in his mind and out of his mind as he pushed himself from the wagon and went over the side of the ledge, not looking at Brazil, but hearing suddenly a hoarse yell as he hit the slope falling, sliding, raising dust, the abrupt leg shock of reaching the bottom, and now rolling and hearing another yell from above and another and lunging into the brush as a shotgun blast ripped the mesquite branches above him.

He was on his feet, running, stumbling through the scrub pine, then suddenly, instinctively, swerving to the left and the shotgun roared again, spattering buckshot through the trees behind him and it went through his mind: Where's the Winchester!

But he did not look back. Coming out of the trees he hesitated, but only momentarily, only long enough to be sure of his direction. His shoes dug into the loose sand and he sprinted down the open hillside, his shoulders drawn tight waiting for the gunfire.

Then it came, the whining report and sand kicking up behind him, and he knew the Winchester was at work. Three times the .45–70 slugs whined ricocheting after him; then stopped abruptly as he reached the dense trees at the bottom of the grade. Silence followed.

He stood for a moment making himself breathe in and out slowly, then started up the slope, up through heavy timber, knowing he would not be seen now. At the top of the ridge he stopped again and this time looked back.

Far across, the wagon was a small shape on the hillside. He could make out men standing behind the wagon, but he could not distinguish one from another or even count how many were standing there. His gaze dropped down the slope, following the course he had taken, but there was no movement anywhere. Minutes went by as he waited and listened, but still there was no movement, nor the sound of anyone coming up through the trees.

Now they'll put the trackers to work, Bowen thought . . . and Brazil probably already halfway there to get them.

His only chance was to make his way back to the Pinaleño station and somehow get a horse. He knew this; and he knew that he had little time before Renda's detachment of Apache police would be reading his tracks.

THREE

WILLIS FALVEY dismounted in front of the Pinaleño adobe. There was no sound in the sunlit yard. His gaze went to the stable shed, then back to the screen door of the adobe. He hesitated uncertainly before going inside.

"Demery?"

There was no answer. His eyes moved from one end of the low-ceilinged room to the other, past Demery's open roll-top desk, past the plank table where the stage passengers ate to the small mahogany-stained bar. The dimness was a relief after the outside glare. It was quiet here, restful, and momentarily it occurred to Willis Falvey that perhaps he might stay here instead of riding all the way to Fuegos.

No, he thought then. He would want to remain all night, and that could prove embarrassing. Not like at Fuegos where he could drink all he wanted in the privacy of a hotel room—in what passed for a hotel room—then sleep it off.

Well, he could have one here . . . at least one. He called for Demery again, waited, then walked to the bar and poured himself a whisky. This would be the start. Perhaps by this evening he would have forgotten, for a time, Frank Renda and the convict camp and his wife, Lizann.

A horse whinnied—the sound coming from the backyard where the corral was located—then Karla's voice.

Falvey listened, then drank down the whisky. He left the bar, walked through the kitchen, and from the back door saw Karla outside. She was rubbing down one of the relay horses in the shade of the long, main stable that extended out from the back of the adobe almost to the corral.

Willis Falvey's eyes raised suddenly. No, there was nothing there; but for a moment he thought he had seen someone standing on the far side of the mesquite-pole corral.

"Karla."

She looked up, seeing Falvey coming out from the adobe, his gaze shifting now and again to the corral. He was unnaturally conscious of himself, she knew, and he had to be occupied when he thought someone was looking at him—even if it was only to glance at corralled horses. The few times he had been here before, Karla noticed this—his obviously self-conscious actions, his almost complete lack of anything to say—and in a way she felt sorry for him. He was out of place at the convict camp, especially as government superintendent, and Karla was sure he realized it more than anyone else.

"Just passing by, Mr. Falvey?"

He nodded, and hesitated before saying, "I helped myself to a drink. I'll put the money on the bar when I go back in. I heard you out here and—"

"That's all right," Karla said easily. "You could pay the next time for that matter."

"I didn't see your father inside."

"He had to go to Fuegos." She said then, "Your friend Renda was here to pick up supplies. I suppose you passed him coming in."

"No, I didn't."

"They only left about an hour ago."

"I took the horse trail," Falvey said. Then asked, "Are you alone?"

She nodded, seeing his gaze move to the corral again.

"I thought I saw someone out there," Falvey said, "just as I came out of the house."

Karla looked out from the shade. "I don't know who it would be."

"No, it was probably the way the horses were standing." Falvey was silent for a moment. "You're here all alone?"

"I'm used to it," Karla said. "Pa has to go to Fuegos every once in a while, to the telegraph office."

"Oh—" Falvey nodded. "What about your mother ... is she—"

"Dead?" Karla smiled at his uneasiness. "No, she's in Willcox with my two sisters."

"I didn't know you had sisters."

"Younger ones. They're still in school and my mother stays with them for the term. They'll be back soon for the summer."

Falvey seemed more relaxed. "It must be hard not seeing them most of the year."

16

"It is, but my mother says we all have to be educated. She was born in Sonora ... You see, her mother was Mexican, but her pa was an American, a mining man, and she didn't go to school at all. That's why we have to, even if it means being away."

"She must be a fine woman."

Karla grinned. "I like her."

"Listen," Falvey said eagerly. "Why don't you come inside while I have a drink?"

"I don't serve the bar, Mr. Falvey."

"I didn't mean that. Just ... so we can talk."

"There's a stage due just before eleven and the change team's not nearly ready."

"It'd only be ten minutes." Falvey smiled. He was trying to make the proposal sound offhand.

"I'm sorry," Karla said. "There's just not time."

"Oh, come on." He was still smiling as he reached out to take her hand, but she stepped away from him. For a moment he stood awkwardly, his arm still extended, then moved toward her again.

Karla backed away. "Maybe you've already had too much to drink."

Falvey stopped. "Karla ... I swear, I only want someone to talk to."

"And I told you I didn't have time."

"Karla—" He hesitated, but stepped toward her again as he said more calmly, "Didn't you ever want to relax and talk to someone? Just talk about anything, as long as it wasn't important. Even the weather. I mean talk without raising your voice, without arguing, without knowing someone's going to snap the next thing you say." He paused. "That's all I want to do, just talk."

"Don't you talk to your wife?" Karla asked hesitantly.

"Have you ever?"

"Talked to her? A few times. But I don't know your wife very well."

"You're fortunate," Falvey said.

Karla stared at him. "I think you'd better go."

"Karla, you don't understand."

"Mr. Falvey, I'm not going to stand here and discuss your wife with you."

"I'm sorry, I shouldn't have said what I did. I started wrong."

17

"Why don't you go in and serve yourself?" Karla said. "I'll come in when I can."

Falvey nodded. "All right." He asked then, hesitantly, "We can be friends, can't we?"

The girl smiled uneasily. "I don't have any enemies, Mr. Falvey."

"Damn it, just say yes or no!"

Karla's eyes showed irritation, and suddenly, anger. "You don't *force* friendship! It either happens or it doesn't happen!"

"I'm sorry—"

"I'm not even sure," Karla said, "I know what you're looking for."

"I'm looking for someone who acts like a human being! Is that too much to ask for?"

"It is when you ask like that!"

"I'm sorry, Karla." He seemed suddenly very tired. "I'm really sorry. I didn't mean to talk the way I did."

"That's all right."

"I'll come back some other time...if it's all right with you."

She nodded, then watched him turn and walk back to the adobe. A moment later she heard his horse, the sound fading into the distance.

The yard was quiet.

Then, as she turned to the horse again, an arm came around her shoulders, jerking her off balance, and a hand covered her mouth before she could cry out. She struggled, her nails digging into the arm across her chest, trying to twist away, trying to turn to see who it was, then glimpsing the bare sun-blackened upper arm close to her face she stopped struggling.

She could feel his arm relax. His hand loosened on her mouth, then came away slowly, brushing her lips.

"Don't call out." His voice was quiet, close to her face. Karla nodded her head and the hand dropped to her shoulder.

"I'm going to take this horse. You just stand still."

Karla nodded again. "All right, Mr. Bowen."

The hands on her shoulder tightened suddenly and pulled her around to face him. "How'd you know who I was?" His face showed open surprise.

"I...recognized your arms."

18

"My arms?"

"From this morning."

"But how do you know my name?"

Karla half smiled. "Mr. Renda told us." She added quickly, "You jumped off at the grade, didn't you?"

"Before that."

"And they couldn't chase you because of the other prisoners."

"That's right."

"But the trackers are probably already following."

"That's right," Bowen said again. Still he did not move. His hands were on her shoulders and he continued to study her dark face, trying to understand the calm way she looked up at him.

"Then you'd better hurry," Karla said. "The saddle's on the wall behind you."

Bowen turned, almost reluctantly. He bridled the big mare, spread the blanket, and as he swung the saddle up, Karla started to walk away.

"Where're you going?"

Karla looked back. "To get you some clothes.' She waited as he stared at her and she felt that she could almost read his thoughts. "Don't you trust me?"

"I don't know why I should."

"All right, ride around with those numbers on your pants."

Bowen shook his head. "I don't understand you."

"What would you like to know?" Karla asked.

"Why're you helping me?"

"I'm not. You're taking a horse. What good would it do if I objected?"

"The clothes—"

"You would have thought of it sooner or later," Karla said. "Hurry now."

Unexpectedly, Bowen said, "Was Falvey bothering you?"

Karla smiled again. "Maybe you're not in a hurry."

"Was he?"

"Mr. Falvey was looking for a friend, that's all."

"He could use one."

"So could you."

"I was trying to figure," Bowen said hesitantly, "if there was something between you."

"You'd better think about getting something between

you and Renda's trackers." She turned. This time he did not stop her and she went on to the adobe.

Bowen was leading the horse out when she returned carrying a blanket roll. "Shirt and pants are inside," Karla said. "And something to eat."

Bowen's eyes remained on her. "I'd like to know why you're doing this."

"I'm not sure why myself," Karla answered quietly. She said then, "If you're caught, they'll make it hard for you."

"Like what, working on a road?"

Karla hesitated. "Did you really steal cattle?"

"Now how would you know that?"

"That doesn't matter now. Just tell me."

"Why would you think I didn't?"

Karla's shoulders moved, her dark eyes still watching him. "I just have a feeling you didn't."

"You can sure simplify things," Bowen said.

"But did you?" Karla asked again.

"I got to go."

"Tell me!"

Bowen swung up to the saddle, then looked down at her.

"That man with the beard this morning—Earl Manring —he hired me in Prescott to help him drive a herd, even showed me a bill of sale for the stock. But the second day out we were arrested to stand trial for rustling. The man who'd sold Earl the stock said he never did such a thing and that the bill of sale Earl had was no good, and he said he could prove it because there wasn't any copy of the transaction in his books."

Karla said, "Didn't you have a lawyer?"

"The court appointed one. We didn't have any money for our own."

Karla frowned. "But the man who sold you the stock—"

"Sold Earl the stock—Earl already had the bill of sale when I met him. The man's name was McLaughlin. He took an oath that he'd never seen the bill of sale Earl had before in his life.

"Earl told me he should've known better than to deal with a man he didn't know, and no wonder the stock was offered at such a good price. He said McLaughlin took advantage of him—got his money for the stock, then didn't register it in his books, called out the law, then even got his stock back. We were arrested one day, tried the next,

20

and there wasn't anything we could do about it. The fastest trial I ever heard of."

"And," Karla said, "you were sentenced to Yuma."

"Seven years each."

"You needed a good lawyer," Karla said thoughtfully.

"We needed more than that."

"You needed a lawyer like Mr. Martz, the Hatch & Hodges attorney. He's in Prescott. He's—" She stopped abruptly, looking up at Bowen.

Bowen shook his head. "The trial's over."

"But if he could prove you didn't know anything about it—"

"He'd be awful good." Bowen reined the mare around. "I hope I can pay you back for this."

"Don't worry about that now."

He looked down at her and seemed reluctant to leave, then said, "Goodbye, Karla." That was all.

She watched him circle the corral and disappear into the pines and only then did it occur to her that he knew her name. He could have heard Renda say it—that was it. But he remembered it—that was the important thing.

FOUR

SALVAJE, sergeant of Apache police, waited. His eyes, beneath the broad hatbrim, were fixed on the dark rise of pines miles to the east—the hillcrest that overlooked the Pinaleño station. He had sent one of his Mimbres there within minutes of being told of the escape. It was something he always did; for invariably the sign led to Pinaleño. With the rest of his trackers he had followed the escaped man's trail to this point. If the signal did not come from the pines, they would continue. Sometimes it took a complete day to bring back an escaped man, but seldom longer than that.

And sometimes it was almost too easy. At least this one had not tried to cover his trail. Some of them used devices that only wasted their time: back-tracking and stream-wading tricks that even a reservation child could understand. Doing this even when their objective was almost always Pinaleño and a horse.

But one had to admit that this was better than duty at San Carlos: the endless hunting of tulapai stills and carrying back men of your own people who had jumped the reservation. Here, one had the opportunity to track white men. Salvaje's father had been a Mimbreño war chief; his mother, a Mexican woman taken in a raid on a Chihuahua pueblo. Salvaje had spent the better part of his life making war against his mother's people and against white men— the good years of riding with Victorio and Delchay, years that could not be compared with this business of recapturing escaped prisoners.

He waited patiently, one thumb hooked in the cartridge bandoleer that crossed his worn cavalry jacket. He was confident that the signal would come, that it was only a matter of time. What else could an escaped man do but go to Pinaleño?—if he had thought about it at all.

And finally the signal did come—a white-gleaming dot in the pines, then the pinpoint flashes, sunlight reflected on a metal disk and sent to him here, miles away, and what Salvaje had known all along was now confirmed.

22

It blinked once; then three times in quick succession. The escaped man had left the adobe and was riding to the west. His man in the pines would follow now and signal again if the escaped one changed direction.

Salvaje looked at his men. There were ten trackers here, and now he watched them remove their army-issue shirts and pants, stripping to breechclouts, then slipping on their cartridge bandoleers again. All of them wore curl-toed Apache moccasions folded and tied just below the knee; and to a man they carried single-shot Springfield carbines.

When they were ready, Salvaje nodded, and they moved off to take the escaped man.

Now the sun was directly overhead. Bowen urged the mare over a cutbank, leaning back in the saddle as the crusted sand gave way and followed them down the slope in a thin dust trail. He entered the cover of trees that grew thickly along both sides of the dry creek bed: cottonwood and sycamore and higher up, farther down the draw, black patches of pine shadowing steep shelfrock. In the dimness it seemed more quiet and he stopped to listen before crossing the creek bed to follow its course through the draw.

He moved carefully, knowing that he was leaving a trail, but more concerned with what might lie ahead than what might be following. Coming this way, he knew, would give the Mimbre trackers time to cut him off. Still, this was wild climbing country, laced with draws and heavy timber to use for cover. South and east from the Pinaleño station were desert flats, and water only if you knew the location of the wells.

Less than two hundred yards farther on, the draw widened and began to rise and here the trees ended. Bowen edged the mare close to the near wall of shelfrock, then moved out into the open and climbed the rise. He stopped then and looked back, down over the green rolling carpet of the treetops.

At first he wasn't sure. Then there was no mistaking it—a thin wisp of dust hanging motionless over the far end of the draw.

His gaze came back to the long sweep of meadow in front of him. It sloped gradually and narrowed into a trough between two pine-studded hills. He would be in the open for more than a mile. But, he thought, trying to keep him-

23

self calm, trying to ignore the uncertainty that was tightening inside of him: You go that way or you don't go at all.

Then the wind was in his face and the mare was pounding over the thick grama grass, racing for the bottom of the meadow. The trough between the hills, perhaps a hundred yards wide, opened before him as he heeled the mare again and felt her lengthen her stride reaching level ground again.

And suddenly, with the high whining report, with the solid smacking sound of the bullet, the mare went down and Bowen was over her head—rolling, stumbling, coming to his feet as the Mimbre rode out of the pines high up on the right slope, then seeing the Mimbre and runing hard for the opposite grade, a shot ringing behind him, then another, and he knew he would not reach the trees.

He veered sharply, running now for an outcropping of rocks at the foot of the hill, hearing suddenly the sound of horses rumbling down the far slope. Three shots sang off the rocks as he went down behind them, and abruptly he heard the horses being reined in. Then silence.

Bowen came up slowly. He brought his knees under him, but kept his head low as he separated the brush that was thick between the rocks.

The Mimbreños were off perhaps eighty yards: eleven of them, all armed and sitting their short, close-coupled horses patiently, taking their time now, as much time as they wanted, to study the rocks. Bowen watched them, wondering why they waited.

If you could think like an Apache, Bowen thought now, you'd know why. All right, then think like a white man. What would you do if you were eleven people and you had one man cornered out in the middle of nowhere? I'd march my eleven people over and drag him out. Eleven what look like Springfields are a match for a pair of bare hands any day of the week and twice on Sunday.

If you're sure they're bare hands.

They know you're not armed.

But that's one of those things you can know and still want to be clearly sure of. So you'd spread out your eleven people and edge in a step at a time and call out things about coming out with your hands up and not trying any funny business.

24

Only you never in your life heard of an Apache doing anything like that, so you can cross that off and throw it away.

But however they do it, they'll try to take you alive. Even if they didn't work for Renda they'd do that. Only— and there're a lot of onlys—they can take you back in all kinds of states where you'd still be alive, though you'd just as soon be dead.

Give yourself up, he thought. No . . . let them work a little bit. You never know what can happen . . . like getting one of their horses.

How do you do that?

How do you do anything! Just shut up and watch!

Not expecting it, he saw one of the Mimbres ride off from the others. His horse went into a canter heading toward the narrowing of the trough between the two hills. Suddenly then, he turned a tight circle, kicking his horse to a gallop, and he came on a dead run directly for the rocks. Bowen went down and the Mimbre passed within ten yards of him firing his Springfield as he went by.

Bowen came up cautiously. He watched the rider circle wide returning to the rest of the band and as he did another Mimbre rode out. This one also pointed off toward the narrowness, giving his horse room to run before coming around, before making his pass at the rocks. He fired as he went by, the shot glancing off rock and whining up into the trees that were high on the slope behind Bowen.

Now, watching the third Mimbre make his circle, Bowen thought: They're making a game out of it, trying to scare you. They've got all the time in the world, so they'll play with you a while—knowing they can take you any time they feel like it. And each one comes a little closer.

He went down as a Springfield roared five yards in front of him, then came up again to watch the Mimbre rejoin the others.

That's some game, he thought then. You know who the winner is before you start. But if you had a gun . . . if you had a gun you could play with them. You could make it a two-sided game. And it occurred to him then: Why didn't you get a gun from her! Clothes and a horse, but no gun.

The fourth Mimbre started to make his circle and Bowen eased down. Or, he thought, get a gun from one of them.

Just like that. Go out and grab onto a Springfield as it goes by.

You've done crazier things. Jumping off that wagon didn't make sense either . . . at first.

He thought of breaking off a mesquite branch to use as a club, but he knew he would never get close enough to use it. Not against a mounted man. No, it had to be something to throw. Something light enough to throw, but hard enough to drop a man from a running horse.

They were scattered all around him, the stones and the broken chunks of rock; but he had had to think in terms of a throwing weapon before becoming fully aware of them. The hoofbeats grew louder as his hand groped for a piece of rock, found one the size of a man's fist, jagged and uneven, and the next moment he was standing, seeing the Mimbre low on the horse, guiding it with his knees, raising the carbine, using both hands and pressing his face close to the breech—

Bowen threw the rock and went down. The carbine exploded over his head and he was up again as the Mimbre looked back, circling toward the others. He had thrown too quickly.

He saw the Mimbre who had just made the pass pointing toward him and a faint sound drifted across the openness. Now they've got something to laugh about, Bowen thought. Something to make the game better. Well, come on. If you think it's funny, keep trying.

He went down, his hand searching for another rock as the fifth Mimbre circled wide to make his pass. But this time, Bowen continued to think, we'll do it different. We'll make up new rules.

He found the right-sized rock, then moved over and away from the boulders almost five yards. Here they was less protection, but enough low brush to cover him. The rider would not see him until he was directly in front of the brush, and then it would be too late to do anything about it.

Now he could hear the Mimbre coming, the quick sound of the hoofs growing steadily. Bowen crouched, judging the distance by the sound. Almost to the rocks, getting ready, bringing up the carbine. Now. He was firing as Bowen came up, rushing past as Bowen hurled the rock, and starting to look back as it caught him in the face.

The Mimbre went back out of the saddle and Bowen was through the brush running for the carbine, picking it up and swinging it suddenly as the Mimbre started to rise. The stock caught the Mimbre's head and he crumpled. Bowen was on him, pulling the bandoleer up over his shoulder; but firing broke suddenly from the other slope and he knew there wasn't time to take the belt. His fingers snatched cartridges from the belt loops and again he was running for the rocks. The firing stopped abruptly as he reached cover.

He looked out again, pushing a cartridge into the breech of the Springfield, then placed the other four cartridges he had taken on a shelf of level rock next to him.

It wasn't even worth it, Bowen thought. Five shots. That's all you've got. What do you do with five bullets against eleven. No, against ten. He looked over to the motionless form of the Mimbre. You should've dragged him back with you. Then you'd have the whole belt ... And you'd have a sore-headed 'Pache to watch.

No, it wouldn't have made any difference. What would you do, shoot all eleven of them? You don't run away from jail because you shouldn't be there in the first place, but kill eleven men doing it. Then you might just as well stay in prison.

You're all mixed up, aren't you? You got yourself into something and now you don't know how to get out.

Maybe scatter them and make a run for it, he thought then. He rolled to his side to study the pine stands up on the hill behind him. The trees were green-brown and motionless against the sky.

Only it's a long run for not knowing what's on the other side. What do you do once you get up there?

Then you think of something else. Just take it a step at a time ... you're not going any faster than that.

He rolled to his stomach again and now saw one of the Mimbres leave the band. This one did not move off as if to make a circle, but came directly toward the rocks.

The brave one, Bowen thought, pressing his cheek against the smooth stock of the carbine. Well, give the brave one something to think about.

He squeezed the trigger and the horse went down. The Mimbre rolled clear and ran back to the others. Then, as he reached them, Bowen fired again. Another horse stumbled, sinking to its knees, and the Mimbres were suddenly wheeling their mounts to move out of range.

And as they scattered in momentary confusion, Bowen moved. He snatched up the cartridges and turned from the rocks, running now for the nearest stand of pines that straggled down the slope behind him. Fifty yards to the trees...then the beating of hoofs bearing down on him. He was loading the Springfield as he ran—dropped a cartridge—knew that he was holding only two more in his hand, and jammed one of them into the breech.

He came around, dropping to one knee, and brought up the Springfield. But the Mimbre veered off to the left, aiming his carbine at Bowen with one hand and both fired at the same time, both shots going wide.

Bowen hesitated. He saw the Mimbre rein a tight circle, starting to reload, and then he was running for the Mimbre—seeing the sudden look of surprise on the Mimbre's face, now seeing the horse jump as it was spurred forward —then dodging the horse's head he swung the carbine up at its rider.

The Mimbre swayed in the saddle, dropping his carbine, but he did not go down. He came back at Bowen to run him down, but again Bowen dodged aside. This time he released the carbine as he swung it and the stock slammed against the Mimbre's head knocking him from the saddle.

The horse came about, feeling its rider go off, slowed to a trot, then a walk—then suddenly broke into a run as Bowen swung up on the saddle and pointed the horse slanting across the slope back toward the long sweep of meadow. But he covered barely a hundred yards before the Mimbres were all around him. He reined abruptly to come back on them, but they closed in before he could break through and he was forced to a stop with seven Springfields leveled at him.

The Mimbres dismounted. One of them, on Bowen's left, reached up to drag him from the saddle. Bowen's fist chopped at him viciously and he staggered back. A carbine barrel jabbed into Bowen's right side. He turned his body, swinging a fist back-handed at the Springfield, and as he did a rawhide loop dropped over his head, and before he could free himself of it the line tightened and he was dragged from the saddle.

The Mimbres swarmed over him and the one Bowen had

struck a moment before swung down at him with the butt of his carbine. Bowen rolled and the stock missed him. The Mimbre brought back the carbine to swing it again, but one abrupt, clearly spoken word in the Mimbreño dialect stopped him.

Bowen came to his feet. He looked for the Mimbre who had spoken and saw Salvaje then standing in front of his horse, the reins over his shoulder and hanging down in front of him. He spoke again and the Mimbres near Bowen stepped back from him.

Salvaje continued to stare at Bowen, openly appraising him and for a moment the hint of a smile softened his mouth. He nodded his head then, slowly, as if to say: It was a good game and it is too bad it had to end—

FIVE

AT ONE TIME, the convict camp at Five Shadows had been a cavalry station—founded during the raiding days of Cochise and garrisoned until Geronimo and his renegade Chiricahuas were sent off to Florida. Officers' row, the troopers' barracks, and even the long stable—forming a U around three sides of the quadrangle—were constructed of a double thickness of adobe brick, for although Five Shadows had been designated a temporary station, there was always a feeling of permanency about the Apache campaigns.

It had been deserted for almost seven years when Frank Renda began using it as a camp for his road construction operation.

In appearance, the camp was much the same as it had always been—even to the windmill and the half dozen Apache *jacales* off beyond the stable where the Mimbreño trackers and their families lived. But now a ten-foot barbed wire fence—three feet of it angled to the inside—enclosed the compound. Over the gate a sign read:

CONVICT LABOR CAMP
KEEP OUT
This camp is under the jurisdiction of the U.S. Territorial Government. Unauthorized persons found entering will be fired on without warning.
F. W. Renda Const. Co.

The five separate quarters of officers' row now housed Renda, his five guards, and the government superintendent, Willis Falvey, and his wife. Across the compound, parallel to this adobe, was the stable. The troopers' barracks, in which the convicts were now kept, formed the base of the U and the six doors of this adobe faced directly south to the camp's only gate. Five of the doors entered directly into the long dirt-floor barracks. The sixth door opened into a single room that had originally been part of the barracks, but was now bricked off and did not have a window. This was the punishment cell.

30

At three o'clock Frank Renda rode into the compound. He had been out at the construction site since returning with the supply wagon. But less than a half hour ago, one of the Mimbres had come to him with word that Bowen had been taken. He placed Brazil in charge then and started back to camp, wanting to be there when they brought in Bowen.

Crossing the open yard, he saw Lizann Falvey come out of the stable. He dismounted in front of her and brought his horse into the shade of the wide, open doorway.

"Have a nice ride?"

Lizann shrugged, removing her gloves and not bothering to look at Renda as he spoke. She wore a green riding suit and hat, the hat straight over her eyes and resembling a small derby, and her auburn hair was pulled back severely into a chignon at the nape of her neck.

"I was out on the road," Renda said, "and saw you go by." Beneath the heavy mustache, his lips barely moved. "I thought I told you not to go near there."

She looked at him now; her expression described boredom and even raising her eyes seemed an effort. Still she did not speak.

"So we're not talking today," Renda said mildly.

Lizann shrugged. "There isn't really much point in it."

"We could talk about Willis going to Fuegos again."

"I didn't know he had."

"Maybe," Renda suggested, "Willis's got a woman there."

Lizann looked at him again. "Willis wouldn't know the first thing about getting one."

"He got you."

"Did he?"

"Then you must've got him," Renda said. He nodded thoughtfully, even though he had thought about this before, months before, when Willis Falvey and his wife had first arrived. He had reasoned it out for himself at that time. "Sure," he said now, "you got him . . . seeing him with Washington friends and thinking he was due for something big. I don't blame you, Lizzy." Renda paused. "But why did he end up here?"

"You're talking to yourself," Lizann said.

"Well," Renda shrugged. "It doesn't make much difference how it happened, when you get right down to it. Does

31

it? You're here and there isn't a solitary thing you can do about it."

"Isn't there?" Their eyes held momentarily. Then Lizann turned from him and started across the quadrangle. Renda slapped his chestnut into the stable and caught up with her.

"So you're still after Willis to quit."

She didn't bother to look at him, but she answered, "That isn't any of your business."

"You might think it isn't," Renda said. "I'll tell you this— the only way Willis quits while I'm here is to get carried out feet first."

"I'm surprised you let him go to Fuegos."

"Willis's got to have *some* fun."

"What if he should run away?"

Renda shook his head. "He doesn't even think about it any more."

Lizann said, "You must have someone there to watch him, or you wouldn't be so sure."

"No, Lizzy . . . you know it and Willis knows it, if he runs out on me he's a ruined man. I don't need anybody bird-doggin' him."

"He's already ruined," Lizann replied.

"Let's say he realizes that," Renda said. "He still wouldn't leave you here. See how it is?"

They were almost halfway across the yard when Renda saw the riders out beyond the gate. They were perhaps a quarter of a mile out and walking their horses toward the compound. Watching them, he said, "A man tried to run away this morning."

Lizann looked up, following his gaze. "Good for him."

"That's him they're bringing back."

"And now you'll teach him a lesson."

"Even if I didn't want to," Renda said, "I would."

They went on to the ramada shade of the long adobe and stopped there to watch the Mimbres ride in.

They straggled to almost single file as the guard opened half of the gate for them, then broke into a trot as they passed into the compound, two of the horses carrying double, and now Renda and Lizann could see the man they were leading.

Bowen was on foot, fifteen feet behind the last Mimbre. His hands were tied behind him and a reata extended from his neck to the saddle horn of the rider in front of him. The reata pulled taut as the horse started to trot and Bowen was jerked forward. He stumbled but kept his feet under him and now had to run to keep up with the horse.

Renda stepped out into the sunlight and raised his arm. "Over here!" He glanced back at Lizann. "They haven't missed yet."

Lizann was watching Salvaje, seeing him coming toward them now. "Animal tracks man," she said. Her gaze moved to Bowen then.

He was hatless and from hair to shoes he was covered with a heavy film of dust. She was sure that he had fallen more than once and had been dragged by the horse. The knees were torn from his pants and his shirt was almost in shreds. Dried blood caked the left side of his jaw and his shoulder was bloodstained where he had wiped his face on it. She could picture him doing this, stumbling along in the dust from the horses with his hands tied behind his back.

"Who is he?" Lizann asked, mildly curious.

Renda was watching Salvaje dismount. "Who?"

"The prisoner?"

"Oh...Bowen."

"He looks as if he's already been taught a lesson," Lizann said.

"Only part of one," Renda answered. He yelled to Salvaje then, "Bring him over here!"

A Mimbre pulled loose the honda and lifted the reata loop over Bowen's head, but did not untie his hands. He took Bowen by the arm then and led him to the ramada.

Renda waited. His thumbs were hooked in his belt and he stared at Bowen, studying his face and waiting for Bowen's eyes to drop or look away. But Bowen continued to return his stare and finally Renda asked, "Was it worth it?"

Bowen didn't answer. Then, he tried to turn his head and bring up his shoulder, seeing Renda suddenly shift his weight, but he was not quick enough and Renda's fist slashed backhanded across his face.

Renda's arm dropped slowly. "I asked you a question."

Bowen nodded then. "It was worth it."

"Why?"

"I learned something."

"You're going to learn more before we're through."

33

Bowen said nothing.

"Like your friend Pryde," Renda said. "He learned his before he got off the road."

Bowen shook his head. "He wasn't in on it."

"That's why he went for Brazil."

Now Bowen hesitated. "Ike did that?"

"He tried. He got a Winchester over the head."

"If Brazil hit Ike," Bowen said quietly, "then he rode up to the wagon to do it. Taking it out on Ike because I—"

"Listen! I'm not discussing this with you...I'm *telling* you!"

"And I'm telling you Ike wasn't in on it!"

Renda's fists came up together, up under Bowen's jaw, and as his head snapped back Renda's right hand fell away then swung viciously against Bowen's face. Bowen went down. He rolled to his side painfully, his head resting on the ground.

"Pick him up," Renda said.

Salvaje stooped and slid his hands beneath Bowen's shoulders. Lifting him, he said. "This one fights well...when he has his hands."

Renda looked at the Mimbre sergeant. "Careful now."

"I say what I know," Salvaje answered. "He fought well and deserves better than this."

Renda nodded slowly, thoughtfully, before saying, "I'll tell you something now. You went out of here with twelve horses. You came back with ten. Worry about where you're going to find two horses and I'll worry about this one."

Salvaje shook his head. "You supply horses. We bring back escaped men."

"I think you'd do better," Renda said, "if you'd never learned to talk English." His tone changed suddenly and he pointed a finger at Salvaje. "You're going to find two horses to replace what you lost, or you're going to find yourself back at San Carlos! You savvy that, Mister Indian?"

Salvaje did not answer, but his eyes remained on Renda.

"Now get out of the way," Renda told him. He waited for Salvaje to move, then stepped up to Bowen, rubbing his fist into the palm of his left hand. Suddenly then, he cocked the fist. Bowen started to roll away from it, but as he did Renda's left hand lashed against his jaw.

Lizann watched Bowen as he tried to rise, as he fell back

again and rolled to his stomach. She looked at Renda then to see what he would do.

Renda's glance went to Salvaje. "Pick him up."

With the Mimbre's help, Bowen came to his feet. He stood swaying, as if ready to fall, his head hanging forward, but as Renda swung at him again he rolled with the fist, and suddenly threw himself at Renda, lowering his head to drive against him. Renda went back a half step. He pushed Bowen away from him and moved in with his fists before Bowen could lower his head again. He hit him with both hands—short body jabs that kept Bowen backing away, trying to twist with the jabs, then a hard solid left hand to Bowen's stomach and as he started to fold forward Renda's right hand hammered against his jaw and he went down.

Renda stood over him, his thick chest rising and falling as he breathed. He backed away then and said, "Pick him up."

"Don't you think," Lizann said mildly, "he's had enough?"

Renda looked at her. "Do I tell you how to take care of Willis?"

"You'd like to be able to," Lizann said.

Renda glanced at her leaning against the ramada post. She always seemed to be lounging, watching something going on, but never taking part herself. He turned to Salvaje again. "I said pick him up."

Bowen was again lifted to his feet, but this time staggered and almost went down before Renda could reach him. Renda's hand caught the front of his shirt. He held Bowen momentarily, then dropped his hand as he shifted his weight and he hit Bowen in the face as hard as he could swing his fist.

He stepped back then, his eyes raising from Bowen to Salvaje. "Throw him in with Pryde. They'll think about it over bread and water for a while." He paused. "Say twenty days. That's a good round number."

Lizann watched Renda hand Salvaje a key; then Salvaje made a sign and two of his Mimbres lifted Bowen to his feet. He stood between them, his shoulders raised awkwardly by the support of their hands under his arms. His legs moved as they led him away, following Salvaje, but his head hung heavily, chin against chest, and Lizann realized that he was barely conscious.

Her eyes followed as they took him across the compound to the convicts' barracks, then along the wind-scarred adobe front of it, past five doors to the sixth one, the punishment cell.

She was thinking of her husband, comparing him to this man Bowen, and wondering if he could have taken half the beating Bowen did.

No, Bowen was of a different breed—a man who would undoubtedly again try to escape, even if failure meant another beating and a longer period in the punishment cell. A man, Lizann reflected, who would go to any extreme. Any extreme.

She saw Salvaje open the heavy door, the two Mimbres move inside with Bowen, then reappear, one carrying the length of rope that had fastened Bowen's hands, then Salvaje padlock the door again, and she continued to think of Bowen, though no longer comparing him to her husband.

Pryde sat against one wall, his legs straight out in front of him. Fifteen feet away, Bowen lay on his side, his face resting on the hard-packed dirt floor. Above him was the outline of a window. It had been bricked in, all of it except a narrow space where the top row of bricks would have gone. This opening ventilated the six- by fifteen-foot cell, and now it framed a thin line of outside light, a faint ray that penetrated the dimness of the room to show Pryde's face in a pale streak against the wall.

He waited until Bowen stirred. Then he said, "Corey—" his voice clear in the stillness though it was barely above a whisper.

Bowen raised his head. "Ike . . . is that you?" His face was numb and swollen tight and as he spoke he could not feel his lips move.

"It's me," Pryde said.

Bowen came up on his elbow. "Ike, I'm sorry." His eyes narrowed as if to see through the dimness. "Ike, did you go after Brazil?"

Pryde's head nodded.

"Why'd you do it?"

"I don't know, I saw him trying to bring up that Winchester and I went for him . . . got him off the horse and hit him once, but that's all."

"I'm obliged to you, Ike."

Pryde said nothing.

"And he gave it back to you over the head."

Pryde's eyes moved. "He gave me more than that. When we got back here, Renda said, 'Learn him a lesson,' and Brazil went and got a pick handle to do it with."

Bowen crawled over him. "You hurt bad?"

"I don't know. I can't move my back."

"Your arms are swollen."

"I think I'm swollen about all over." He said then, still calmly, "Listen...you got to know something."

"We have a long time to talk," Bowen said. "Go to sleep now."

"Listen to me!" Pryde's voice rose. But he relaxed again as he said, "After Renda emptied his shotgun, he ran back to where we were. Brazil fired then, but it was too late. I was on the ground and my head buzzed like hell. That's why I'm not sure of the exact words...though the meaning was plain enough."

Bowen shook his head. "I don't follow you."

"You will. Renda looked like he wanted to kill somebody." Pryde went on, "but there wasn't anything he could do. Then he yelled out, 'You said not till the grade!' or words just like that."

Bowen frowned. "He said that to Brazil?"

Pryde shook his head slowly. "To Manring. Somewhere along the line Earl told him you were going to run."

SIX

THEY COUNTED the days by marking the wall with Pryde's belt buckle, a mark for each day scratched in a row on the adobe wall. But even with this, after little more than a week had passed, they were not sure of the count and it seemed there should be more marks on the wall than there were. Twice a day the door opened and they were given bread and water. The guard who carried the bucket and dipper and a half loaf of bread was never armed. But another guard stood in the doorway with a shotgun. They were ordered not to talk to the prisoners and would not answer with even a sign when Bowen or Pryde asked the number of days they had been there.

In the morning, they would hear Renda or Brazil in front of the barracks lining up the convicts for the wagon trip to the construction site. Then, throughout the day, there was silence, long hours of dead silence only occasionally broken by the sound of a horse crossing the compound.

In the evening, after the convicts were in the barracks again, the faint murmur of voices, bits of conversation that were never completely clear, would drift into the darkness of the punishment cell. Bowen would sit with his back against the adobe not moving, listening for Manring's voice. But thinking of Manring, wanted to be sure he would still be here at the end of twenty days, made the time pass even more slowly.

Why had Manring warned Renda that he was planning to escape?

Pryde said, because he's paid for it. He had seen the same thing at Yuma. There were special privileges for the convict who kept the guards informed on what was going on *inside* the cell blocks. And, Pryde said, there was only one way to deal with that kind.

Maybe it was that simple. But Bowen went over in his mind everything he knew about Manring, trying to find a more personal reason.

They had met in a saloon of the Commercial House Hotel in Prescott just a little more than a year ago—Bowen with a trail drive behind him and for the time being nothing to do; Manring looking for a man to help him move a small herd down to San Carlos—the two of them standing at the bar. A few minutes after they started talking, they moved to a table.

"Ordinarily," Manring had explained, "I work for a spread same as anybody else, but I heard about this cry for beef down at San Carlos and saw it was a chance to make something if you had a little capital." And taking a bill of sale out of his pocket—"The reservation's grown bigger than the government beef allowance, so now they got to buy more. But they're buying monthly, just a hundred head or so at a time and it don't pay the big owner to take a herd down there. That's why somebody like you or me can make money out of it if you got stock to sell." He pointed to the bill of sale. "Which I got."

Bowen said it sounded all right to him. He was thinking about going down to Willcox to talk to a friend about a mining venture and if he could work his way down that was all the better.

The next morning they started driving the herd—forty head they had gathered themselves. Bowen noticed none of the steers had been vent-branded and he asked Manring about it.

"Why go to the trouble of registering a brand," Manring answered, "Then waste time putting it on when you'll only have the stock about a week? A bill of sale's good enough to prove ownership."

When Bowen opened his eyes the next morning, a man he had never seen before was standing over him with a rifle. There were eight or ten others in the clearing and a moment later he saw Manring brought in. Manring was mounted and it was evident he had tried to run when the posse closed in.

They were taken back to Prescott and formally charged that afternoon, the complaint being signed by R. A. McLaughlin, the man from whom Manring claimed to have bought the cattle. Luckily (the sheriff said) a district judge would be in Prescott the next day—so there wouldn't be a delay in the trial.

Bowen remembered that first night in a jail cell clearly—watching Manring lying on his bunk smoking and for a long time neither of them spoke. But there were some things Bowen wanted to say and finally—

"If you'd vented McLaughlin's brand at the time of the sale we wouldn't be in jail." He was sorry as soon as he'd said it. That if-talking was like closing the barn after everything had run out. But Manring drew on his cigarette, not bothering to answer, and Bowen could feel his anger begin to rise.

"Why didn't you vent his brand when you closed the deal?"

Manring's head turned on the mattress. "I told you."

"Earl...this McLaughlin said you worked for him once, about three years ago. Took you on for a Kansas drive."

"I heard him."

"You claimed that wasn't so."

Manring stubbed out the cigarette. "You going to do the hearing all over again?"

"Earl"—he remembered that his voice was calm and that he wasn't yet really angry—"did you buy those cattle or did you steal them?"

Manring was on his back, staring at the ceiling. "I don't want to hear any more about it."

"Earl, they're going to try me tomorrow for something I don't know anything about!"

"Have a good cry," Manring muttered.

Bowen rose. "I asked you a question. I want to know if you really bought that stock!"

"So does the judge," Manring said. He started to roll over, turning his back to Bowen, but suddenly Bowen was dragging him up by the arm and as he came off the bunk Bowen hit him. He hit Manring four times before the sheriff's deputy came in to separate them.

The trial began at ten o'clock the next morning. At noon they recessed for dinner and for the jury to reach a decision. Then at two o'clock that afternoon the judge passed sentence. *Seven years in the Territorial Prison at Yuma.* There had been no time wasted. It was McLaughlin's word against Manring's and as far as both the judge and the jury were concerned, this was not a two-sided question. In sentencing them, the judge admitted being lenient, since to his knowledge neither of the accused had a previous criminal record.

That night Bowen and Manring were placed in separate cells to await transportation to Yuma.

For the next nine months, on Prison Hill, Bowen saw Manring every day, but they seldom spoke. He made himself believe that Manring was also innocent. That made it easier to live with him. Still, they had little in common and there was no reason for a friendship to exist between them. Gradually, then, he ceased to even think about Manring and the trial and he began to consider him nothing more than another Yuma convict. Being in different cells—though both were in the main cell block—made it that much easier.

From the first day he entered Yuma, Bowen thought of escape. He had made up his mind that he was not going to pay with seven years for something he didn't do. But thinking of escaping from Yuma you had to consider the Gatling gun over the main gate, the hundreds of miles of desert surrounding the prison, the Pima trackers who would bring you back for a bounty and, finally, the "Snake den" cell in the dungeon block where you would live for a month or more, chained to the stone floor, if the escape failed.

During the time they were at Yuma, construction of the cell block for incorrigibles was still in progress—a project planned to carve a dungeon of twelve cells out of solid granite. Bowen was assigned to the dynamite crew; and it was the experience gained in this work that was primarily responsible for his leaving Yuma some months later.

Their transfer came unexpectedly. Bowen, Manring and four other convicts—one of them Pryde—were taken from their cells one evening soon after supper. Nineteen days later, a wagon rolled through the barbed wire gate of the convict camp at Five Shadows as Frank Renda stood by to greet them.

In their three months here, Bowen had talked to Manring more often; and only a few days before the supply trip to Pinaleño, Manring had hinted at a plan of escape. But by then, Bowen had made up his mind to try it his own way and Manring's hints had been too vague to even arouse his curiosity.

Still, he thought now, Manring had considered him in his escape plan. That was the point. That was the main reason Pryde's story of Manring informing on him left a question in his mind.

41

There were twenty-two marks on the wall the morning Brazil opened the door and told them to come out. As soon as they were outside, both men lifting a hand to shield the sun from their eyes, and unexpectedly noticing the convicts grouped along the front of the barracks watching them, Brazil slammed the heavy door and walked away.

"It's Sunday," Bowen said.

Pryde was looking toward the convicts. "He's not there."

"Let me worry about Manring," Bowen said.

He walked along the front of the barracks, every convict in the yard watching him, and those near him nodded as he approached then moved aside as he entered the barracks. Over the yard there was a silence.

Two convicts playing a card game looked up as he entered. They seemed to hesitate. Then one of them began dealing the cards again. The other convict looked past the dealer, down the length of the adobe, down the row of straw mats that were lined along the wall, before his gaze dropped to the cards again.

Manring was lying on his side, his eyes closed and his left arm pillowing his head. Then his eyes opened, raising from Bowen's shoes up to his face.

"Corey, you look thinner."

Bowen said nothing, but his gaze remained on Manring's bearded face. He heard a step behind and he knew it was Pryde.

"And a few shades paler," Manring said.

There was a momentary silence before Bowen said, "You might be about to get your teeth kicked out."

Manring pushed himself up. "You better go easy." His eyes shifted to Pryde, then to Bowen again. "What for?"

"You told Renda I was going to jump the wagon."

"You figured that out the last twenty days?"

"Ike told me . . . the first day."

Manring's eyes went to Pryde again. "And what exactly did Ike tell you?"

"That Renda said something to you . . . like, 'You said not till the grade.' "

"When was that?"

"Right after I jumped."

Manring's jaw relaxed. "How would Ike know? He'd just had his head busted with a Winchester."

"But he was still awake."

"All right." Manring shrugged. "Maybe Renda said that. I don't know—there was a lot of shooting going on. But if he said it, he didn't say it to me."

"Who would he say it to, Brazil?"

"Who else is there! Listen, you're accusing me of something you don't know anything about. Get your facts straight before you come marching in here like a couple of vigilantes!"

"I got mine straight," Pryde said. "You know it and I know it."

Manring shook his head. "After Brazil busted you, you started hearing things."

"Corey might not be sure," Pryde said. "But I am. I was there. I heard Renda say it right to your face—"

"What did I say to his face?"

Renda stood in the doorway behind them, then came forward a few steps as Bowen and Pryde half turned. "What did I say?"

Pryde shook his head. "Nothing."

"Ike, you want to go back in the closet?"

Pryde did not answer and for a long moment Renda stared at him. His eyes moved to Bowen then. "You two spend three weeks in the house and when I let you out you come right back in." He paused. "You like being inside?" He answered his own question saying, "All right, we'll give you some inside work. Ike, you and your friend Corey go over and clean out the stable. Rub down the horses, too." He turned to go, then looked back. "And Ike...don't come out till the sun goes down."

Lizann Falvey watched her husband finish the whisky in his glass, seeing his hand come down slowly to the table and release the glass almost reluctantly. The table was across the room, at least a dozen feet away, but she could see that the bottle was empty.

Now a trip to Fuegos, she thought. She was sitting in a canvas chair studying Willis and wondering how long he would last.

He'll go to Fuegos to finish what he has started and come back tomorrow with six bottles, three in each saddle bag. You can look forward to that. And in a few days you can look forward to it again. Then again...and again—

She sat and watched him, waiting. Waiting for him to

43

look up from the table, but he continued to study the label of the whisky bottle and finally she said, "Willis—"

His head turned. "What?"

"In the top drawer of my dresser," Lizann said, "there's a gun. I believe you called it a .25-caliber Colt. Why don't you take it and go for a ride up into the hills."

Willis frowned. "What?"

"Or just go behind the adobe," Lizann said. "I thought at first I'd rather not hear the shot, but on second thought it really wouldn't matter."

"What are you trying to say?"

"I'm not *trying* to say anything. I'm telling you to put a gun to your head and be done with it."

The whisky had relaxed him, had made him drowsy and it cushioned, somewhat the shock of her words. His expression scarcely changed.

"You sincerely hate me, don't you?"

Lizann shook her head. "That's putting it too simply. I suppose there are moments when I think I hate you, but most of the time I can feel only disgust. You hate a man like Frank Renda who is strong enough to be hated and you would hate even a memory of him. With your kind, Willis, you feel either sorrow or disgust and when that's passed you're hardly worth a memory—a feeling of indifference at best."

Willis stared. "Why don't you leave me?"

"Don't you think I would if I could?"

"What's stopping you?"

"What's stopping me?" Lizann repeated without tone in her voice. "Willis, I think I'm beginning to feel sorry for you. You don't even fully realize the kind of man you're dealing with. Do you think Frank Renda would let me leave?"

"You go for rides. You could keep going."

"I have never gone out without one of Salvaje's men following me."

"I go to Fuegos," Willis said. "No one follows me."

"Renda doesn't have to watch you. He even admitted that. You're your own watchdog, Willis."

"Renda's very sure of himself."

Lizann shrugged. "He's in a position to be." Her expression softened then. "But, Willis . . . he doesn't have any more on you than you do on him."

"So?"

"So...report him."

"Just like that."

"Be a *man* one time in your life!"

"Which is easy for you to say. But you're not the one that goes to prison."

"You're already in prison. We both are."

"Then," Willis said, "we might as well stay where we are."

Lizann rose from the chair and walked to the window. Her gaze went over the yard to the convicts sitting and leaning against the front of the barracks, then came back as she saw Frank Renda leave the shade of the ramada and start across toward them. Her eyes followed him until he reached the barracks and went in the first door, then she turned to her husband again.

"Are you going to Fuegos today?"

Willis looked up. "I thought I would."

"Willis...when you get there, what would stop you from taking the stage to Tucson?"

His breath came out wearily and he shook his head.

"Listen to me! In Tucson you could write to the Bureau. Within two weeks someone would be here to investigate."

"And two weeks later I'd be in jail."

"No! After you send the letter, go somewhere else."

"Would you meet me?"

Lizann hesitated. "Haven't you had enough of this?"

"If I thought we could start over—"

"There is only one way to do that, Willis. But not together. God knows, not together. Think about getting out of here. Let what comes later take care of itself."

He shook his head then. "Sooner or later I'd be caught. Going to prison is one thing. Perhaps I could take a year or so of it to get out of this mess. But I'd also be killing my career."

"Your career!" Lizann's voice rose. "A bookkeeper in a convict camp! That's your career—that's what your big political friends think of you. They've put you away, out of their hair. Don't you realize that?"

"You didn't think that way a year ago," Willis said.

"I'm talking about now!"

"When you married me," Willis said, "you were sure I had a future. Or else you wouldn't have considered it."

"With a clean collar on," Lizann said, "you can fool almost anyone."

Willis was silent, studying the bottle again. Lizann waited. Finally he looked up. "It wouldn't be worth the chance."

"How do you know, unless you try it?"

He shook his head. "I'd be hiding out the rest of my life."

"I wouldn't," Lizann said calmly. "I'm asking you to do it for me."

He looked at her as if to answer, but his gaze dropped and he pushed himself up from the table. Lizann watched him go into the bedroom and when he reappeared, moving past her without raising his eyes, he was carrying his hat and saddle bags. She saw him hesitate as he opened the door and he turned to her again.

"I'm sorry, Lizann. I'm sincerely sorry."

"For me, Willis...or for yourself?"

"I think for both of us." He stepped outside, closing the door behind him.

Lizann turned to the window again. She was watching her husband cross the yard when Bowen and Pryde came out of the barracks and followed Willis to the stable.

So he's out, Lizann thought. Why couldn't he have been Willis?

No, she thought then. You made the mistake yourself. And you'll live with it the rest of your life unless you do something. You should have been more patient. There were others. But you guessed wrong and picked Willis—who was then what he is now. So you can't really blame Willis.

They had met in Washington less than a year before. Three weeks later they were married. Lizann: a young woman whose father had been killed at Second Bull Run a year after she was born, killed in a cavalry action, leaving wife and daughter a name, but very little money to support the name. And Willis: a young man whose father, also with a name, had also died, leaving his son sole heir to a moderately large estate. But it was not until after their wedding and honeymoon that Lizann learned Willis had gambled away almost his entire inheritance. All that remained were the stories of his fortune—the same stories which had attracted Lizann to him. Still, she was not yet discouraged. Willis did have influential friends. And a political appointment was in the offing. Three months later they were in Prescott. There, Willis was told he would serve "somewhat as a liaison man" between the territorial government, the military and a privately operated road construction project. A few weeks later they were at Five Shadows. After the first day, Lizann fully realized the mistake she had made.

Now she looked out across the yard again to the stable and she thought of Bowen—remembering how she had compared her husband to him the day he was placed in the punishment cell; remembering now how she had catalogued him in her mind: *a man who would do anything to escape.*

She thought of him calmly, impersonally now, feeling that there had been something almost instinctive in choosing him from among all the convicts. As if—since Willis would no nothing—Bowen was the next logical choice to help her.

But how?

In some way that would benefit him. That, she realized already. A way that would help him escape. But, she thought now, talk to him first. He isn't on Renda's side. But neither is he necessarily on yours.

Before leaving the window to change into her riding suit, she saw her husband ride out of the gate. Less than ten minutes later, she walked across the yard and into the wide opening of the stable. She saw Pryde immediately, at the far end sweeping the aisle between the stalls—then Bowen. He was in the first stall on the right side, currycombing Renda's big chestnut mare. She walked toward him.

"Frank didn't waste time putting you back to work, did he?"

Bowen looked up. "No, ma'am." He watched her move toward him. She came almost into the stall, stopping to lean against the end of the partition that separated this stall from the next one. This was the first time she had even spoken to him and her relaxed, almost familiar manner surprised him.

"Will you saddle my horse?"

"All right." He looked back, over the partition. "Which one?"

"The sorrel, on the other side.

Bowen turned, taking a step as he did, then stopped abruptly. Lizann, less than an arm's length from him, had not moved.

47

"I'm in no hurry," she said. "Finish what you're doing."

"I've got all day to do this," Bowen said.

Lizann was studying him openly. "How do you feel?"

"Not so good," Bowen said. Her eyes made him conscious of his three weeks' growth of beard, his ragged, sweat-stained appearance.

"I saw what Renda did to to you," Lizann said quietly. "I was standing behind him."

Bowen nodded. "I noticed."

"It's too bad your hands were tied."

"Maybe it was good. I might have killed him."

"Do you mean that?"

Her question surprised him. "I mean I was mad enough at the time."

Lizann nodded slowly. "I could see why you would be. You've been here, what—three months?"

"That's right."

"And Yuma before that," Lizann said. "With six years yet to serve of a seven-year sentence. I can't say I blame you for trying to escape."

"How do you know all that?" Bowen asked. He was reminded of Karla Demery. Now a second woman who seemed to know all about him.

"I looked up your record," Lizann said.

"For a reason?"

"Perhaps."

"What were you looking for?"

Lizann smiled. "You've a very suspicious nature. Perhaps I just felt sorry for you . . . thought you needed a friend."

Bowen shook his head. "Not in a convict camp. With a husband."

"My husband doesn't know everything I do."

"But Renda does. He has to know what everybody's doing. Even you."

"You sound very sure of yourself."

"What's going on here," Bowen said, "is black and white and you know it as well as anyone else. Renda gets seventy cents a day for each convict—thirty of us—for food, clothes and shelter. But he doesn't spend two bits a man on his best day. He buys cheap flour, full of worms. The coffee goes twice as far as it should. The Mimbres shoot most of his meat which costs him only for bullets. We sleep on straw mats you wouldn't put a dog on. Since I've been here three men have died on those mats. Not one of them had a doctor, though Renda's supposed to provide medical care. He makes money on the road contract and he's keeping it going as long as he can, for every day he can stretch it he makes that much more money off the convicts. Anybody who's been here longer than one day knows it. So it comes down to this—living here you're either his friend or his prisoner and either way he knows what you're doing."

Lizann's eyes remained on him. "You've thought it out very carefully."

"I've had the time."

"Which do you think my husband is, friend or prisoner?"

"Maybe both. But he drinks so he won't have to admit to being either."

"And I?" Lizann asked. "Which am I?"

"Until a while ago, I would've thought you and Renda got along fine."

Lizann's eyebrows raised inquiringly. "And now?"

"Now I'd say you want out."

"You just thought of that," Lizann said. "You're guessing."

Bowen moved his hand slowly over the smooth back of the chestnut. "I'll guess something else."

"I'm listening."

"You're looking for somebody angry enough to help you."

For a moment there was no sound in the stable. They were aware then of the faint sound of Pryde sweeping at the far end, but that was all. Their eyes held, neither of them moving until Lizann asked, quietly, "Are you angry enough, Corey?"

"That all depends."

"On me?"

Bowen nodded. "On what's on your mind."

"I'll be perfectly honest with you," Lizann said softly. She moved closer to him. "I don't know how it can be done. All I know is I have to get away from here. My husband has refused to help me and Renda has me watched constantly. That's why I have no choice but to—"

"Come to a convict."

"I wasn't going to say that. I have no choice but to devise my own means of getting away from here."

"You'd leave your husband?"

"He's already left me, you might say."

"Why won't he help you?"

49

"You said it yourself. He's Renda's prisoner."

"He could get word out somehow," Bowen said. "Mail a report from Fuegos."

"He could...if he wasn't accepting money from Frank."

"Renda's bribing him?"

Lizann nodded calmly. "If he reports Frank, Frank will report him. Staying here, Willis is desperately protecting what he chooses to call his career in government service."

"I didn't think Frank was making that much that he could afford to pay somebody off."

"He doesn't have a choice."

"It seems to me," Bowen said, "he could get away with just threatening your husband."

"Perhaps he could, but it wouldn't be as sure as the way he's doing it."

"How long has your husband been taking the money?"

"I suppose from almost the first day we came here. It wouldn't have taken Willis long to realize what Renda was doing. Willis keeps the books...That's something else, another way Renda has him. All the accounting is in Willis's handwriting—the entries of the government subsistence funds, then the recording of fictitious expenditures to cover the funds going into Renda's pocket. As far as the people in Prescott know, the convicts are getting the equivalent of seventy cents a day—in food, clothing, blankets... well, you know, you mentioned it a moment ago."

"How much does your husband get out of it?"

"I don't know. Perhaps just enough to cover the six bottles of Green River he buys every week."

"Maybe Renda forced him into it somehow."

"I have found," Lizann said quietly, "that worrying about my husband serves no one's purpose, not even his."

Bowen studied her thoughtfully. "All right...now tell me where I fit in."

"I'm not yet sure," Lizann answered. Her face was raised to his and for a moment neither of them spoke. "But," she asked then, "you'd be willing to help me, wouldn't you?"

"It still depends," Bowen said mildly. "You tell me when you think of a way to leave...and then I'll let you know."

SEVEN

By FIVE THIRTY A.M. the roving night guard had made his
last swing through the compound, checked with the gate
guard and had gone to wake up the cook. Fifteen minutes
later, Renda and the day men were up and dressed. They
unlocked one door of the barracks, brought the convicts
out single file and counted them before marching them to
the outside mesquite-pole-awninged mess tables behind
the barracks.

At six o'clock they were lined up in front of the barracks
again. A few minutes later, three single-team wagons moved
out of the compound—the first carrying equipment, the
other two, the convicts. A guard rode alongside both of the
convict wagons and Renda and Brazil brought up the rear.
As the wagons rolled through the gate, twelve Mimbreño
trackers rode out from their camp. Three of them held
back to follow the wagons, but the rest went on, spreading
out and running their horses now toward the looming sand-
colored slope less than a mile in the distance. As the sun
rose higher, five shadow lines formed by washes and rock
slides would creep down the slope like a gigantic hand
groping for the convict camp below.

In the third wagon, sitting next to Bowen, Pryde
said, "There they go. You see them in the morning, then
you see them maybe once all day."

"Unless," Bowen said, "you try to run. Then you see
them again." He watched Salvaje, a good fifty yards out,
ride by the wagons, and he nodded, saying to Pryde, "How'd
you like to have him on our side?"

Pryde turned to watch the Mimbres. "That would do it,
wouldn't it?"

That would do it all right, Bowen thought—his eyes raising
to Renda and Brazil who had separated and dropped back
a dozen yards or more to be clear of the dust rising from
the wagons—once you got by those two. Maybe, he continued to think, there's where Lizann comes in. To help you
get by.

51

But how does a woman help you break out of a convict camp?

No—don't underestimate her because she's a woman. Not that one. And don't think she's doing it for you. You guessed it and she admitted it. She wants out. She wants to be free of Renda ... and the wire fence and the Mimbres and the sun and ... even if it means running away with a convict she doesn't know from any other convict. Think about that. Think about it good and see what it tells you. A woman who's willing to leave her husband behind ... willing to help a convict if he'll help her. Picture the way she was in the stable and the way she spoke, then add. Add it up without cluttering it with running-hiding-making-it-escaping-from-it pictures and see what you get. Put yourself in her shoes. Be sick of your husband and hating Renda and hating everything in sight. Then look at you. A weapon. Somebody Renda beat hell out of. Somebody angry enough. You said it yourself. You don't have to reason it out. You said it yourself in the stable. Somebody angry enough. She'll use you for a battering ram to bust the door down. That's all. If you can get up and run out yourself, all right. If you can't, she's not going to stop to help you up. And if she fails, then it was a convict who forced her into it.

And so you know all that just by looking at her face, guessing what wasn't said but what was almost said. Is that how you know all about her?

Yes. Some things you know.

Some things are very simple and you can take all this reasoning that really isn't reasoning and throw it out because you knew with the first word she said and the way she said it that she was after something and if she wanted it bad enough she'd get it, one way or another. With you or with somebody else. And knowing it you'll go along with her, because at least it's a chance and one chance is better than six more years of this. Even if you don't make it.

So what have you got?

He was still watching Renda and he thought: Ride over here close and look the other way and let that shotgun barrel stick out a little more.

Then get Brazil first.

Yes, that's smart thinking. Ask Pryde if he thinks that's

cool, calm, smart thinking. Ask him if he *feels* anything about it.

If you planned a break with one of the convicts, he wouldn't think of *you,* would he? He's think of himself. And you'd think of *your*self. That's what it comes down to. She's as much a prisoner as anyone else. So if she wants to get out, even needing somebody else, she'll be thinking of herself. It's not surprising now, is it? Suddenly it's not surprising. Your mistake was thinking of her as a woman instead of as another convict.

So forget she's a woman and just listen to whatever she has to say. Forget she's supposed to think like a woman, however women are supposed to think. She's another convict. Put a convict's shirt on her and numbered pants if that makes it any easier.

He began to picture Lizann in a man's shirt, not doing it intentionally, but because it was already in his mind; but suddenly the woman was no longer Lizann and he was picturing Karla Demery in a faded blue chambray shirt, the one she had been wearing that day three weeks ago.

As the trail began to climb, Bowen watched Brazil come up almost to their wagon before turning his horse from the trail. He rode even with them then, but off beyond the twisted, shaggy-barked cliff rose bushes that grew close along the wagon ruts. Renda remained behind, though he seemed to be closer to the wagon now. The three Mimbres who had trailed him were no longer there.

Then, watching Renda, Bowen thought of Karla Demery again—picturing her with Renda in the station yard. Then later, when he had been close to her—

Her short black hair making her look almost like a boy yet, strangely, more feminine because of it. A slim body. Small even features. Clean-scrubbed, clean-smelling and dark from the sun, though you knew some of the warm brown was Mexican blood and you could see it in the eyes—one quarter from her mother's side. Not more than one quarter. In the eyes that were alive and didn't move from your face as you spoke, though not the way Lizann Falvey's had not moved.

Read Karla, Bowen thought. Not the giving you the clothes and the horse and the talking about the lawyer. Read what was behind her eyes the way you did Lizann's. If you can do that, you'll understand the horse and the clothes and the other thing. But it isn't as easy, is it? You don't just label her and say, There, that's why she's doing it.

Which one would you rather be with?

For what?

For anything!

You almost kissed her.

You almost kissed both of them.

No...Karla. You almost climbed right off the horse to kiss her. Not for what she had done but because you *wanted* to. The other was different. Lizann was trying to make you kiss her. But you didn't.

Maybe you should've gotten off the horse.

The wagons followed a dry wash down through rock-strewn, pinyon-studded talus to the wide floor of a canyon and here intersected the new road that, following the canyon, came down from the north. The wagons moved down canyon a good three hundred yards before halting at the end of construction.

Bowen waited his turn, then jumped down from the wagon. Pryde followed him. They started for the equipment wagon as Brazil rode up.

"You two unhitch the team."

Pryde looked up at him. "We're going to pull stumps?"

Brazil grinned. "Till your back breaks."

They watched Brazil ride on to the equipment wagon. "I knew we'd be pulling stumps," Pryde said.

"One job's as bad as another," Bowen said. He looked back along the new road. "We didn't miss very much. That needle rock back there. We were even with it three weeks ago."

Pryde squinted along the canyon. "Maybe two and a half miles."

"Renda's making it last," Bowen said.

Pryde nodded. "Four months to come about twelve miles and not doing much more than cutting a path."

"With another four miles to go," Bowen said. He turned to look down the canyon. "The hardest four. Up over the rocks, then down to come out somewhere behind the stagecoach station. Renda can make that last a good two months."

"He must know somebody," Pryde said.

Bowen nodded. "He'd have to. He doesn't know anything about road building."

"The government must have lots of money," Pryde said thoughtfully. "Six months to build sixteen miles of road through the mountains to save one day's travel from Willcox to San Carlos."

"To save a half day," Bowen corrected. "You *know* Renda knows somebody."

Brazil motioned to them and they brought the team up past the equipment wagon where two convicts stood waiting for them. One, a Mexican, with a twelve-foot length of chain over his shoulder; the other leaning on a long-handled shovel. Bowen nodded to them.

The convict with the shovel squinted as if he needed glasses and the lines of his face formed a nervous, half-smiling expression. He was a small man, perhaps forty. His straw hat was cocked over one eye and his shirt collar was buttoned, though it hung loosely, at least three sizes too large for him, and he gave the impression that even in convict clothes he was trying to keep up his appearance—the white collar, coat and tie appearance of a man who had been an assistant cashier at the Wickenburg bank until the day he stole five hundred and fifty dollars to cover a gambling debt. His name was Chick Miller; the man who had described the supply wagon trip to Bowen.

"Corey," he said now, "I'm sorry you didn't make it." When Bowen said nothing, he added, "I hope you don't hold it against me."

"Why should I?"

"I mean since I was the one told you to try it."

"I made up my own mind," Bowen said.

Chick grinned. "Brazil came riding like hell through here to gather the trackers and we thought for certain you'd made it."

"Chick, did you tell Earl I was going to try it?"

The question came unexpectedly and Chick Miller straightened, his hands sliding down the handle of the shovel. "Why would you think that?"

"Just tell me if you did."

"Of course not!"

"Chick, I don't care if you did."

"Maybe he saw us talking."

Bowen nodded. "Or maybe you suggested he try it."

"I might have done that."

"Then told him I was going to."

"Why would I do that?"

"Chick, I'm not holding it against you if you did. I just want to know."

"I might've mentioned you were thinking about it." Chick Miller shook his head then. "But I wouldn't have come right out and *told!*"

The Mexican, a young, clean-shaven, dark-skinned man, said, "That's why I don't even think about it. You get it in your mind to run and everyone knows about it."

Chick Miller looked at the Mexican. "You keep out of what don't concern you." He stopped then, seeing Brazil riding toward them.

Brazil pulled up, his Winchester across his lap and pointing at them. "Just passing the time of day?"

Chick Miller grinned. "We're waiting for the axe crew to give us some work."

Brazil nodded to a tree stump just beyond them. "There's one left from Saturday. Start on it."

"That one won't be in the roadway," Chick Miller said.

Brazil studied him. "You going to argue over it?"

"I just thought, why pull her out if she's going to be off the road anyway." He saw Brazil start to dismount and the half-smiling, squinting expression came over Chick's face. "I mean it's not going to be in the way."

Brazil swung down and started for him. He waved the barrel of the Winchester at the other three men and said, "Get out of the way," not taking his eyes from Chick.

"We'll take her out," Chick said. He glanced at the Mexican, seeing him move away; then to Bowen and Pryde who were watching Brazil and now he saw them back away slowly. As he turned to Brazil again the Winchester barrel was swinging toward him. He threw up his arms and fell back stumbling but keeping his feet and the barrel slashed past his head. Chick started to run.

"Stand where you are!"

He stopped, but seeing Brazil coming toward him again, began to back away.

"I said stay where you are!"

Chick held up his hand. "I don't want to get hit. Listen, we'll pull the stump. Just let me get my shovel." His extended hand pointed. "I dropped it over there." His eyes opened wide as Brazil moved toward him and at that moment he turned to run, taking one stride as the rifle barrel slammed across his back and he went down covering his head with his arms.

Brazil looked down at Chick, then turned from him. "Now pull the stump," he said.

The Mexican went to Chick and kneeled over him. Bowen watched Brazil mount and ride down canyon. There, twenty yards ahead of them, a half dozen convicts were clearing the pinyon clumps: cutting the trees close to the ground, but leaving enough stump for the chain to be wound around and fastened to securely.

As the Mexican helped Chick to his feet, Pryde and Bowen walked over to them. Pryde asked, "How are you?"

An exaggerated expression of pain was on Chick's face, "He'll be sorry he did that."

Pryde shook his head. "When the time and the day comes, you'll be second in line. I got first dibs on Mr. Brazil."

The Mexican was looking at Pryde. He smiled then. "If that day ever comes, I hope I'm there to see it. When you're through with him, maybe I'll kick him in the face."

By noon, they were not more than a hundred yards farther down the canyon. The convicts worked as slowly as Renda would let them, knowing that he wanted to stretch the job time for all it was worth. Still, two or three times a day Renda would conscientiously speed up the work pace, as if rebelling against this one small advantage they held over him.

The clearing crew would cut down the pinyon and large mesquite bushes, drag them to the side of the canyon and burn them. The stump-pulling crew followed—digging under the shallow-rooted pinyon stumps, looping the chain about the trunk stub, levering with the shovel and finally pulling it out with the wagon team. One of them would drag the stump to the nearest fire as the others went on to the next stump.

Two guards watched the clearing crew because there was usually thick brush ahead of them. From the east side of the canyon, Brazil watched the group Bowen was with, and most of the time Brazil did not leave the thin strip of shade close to the slanting talus wall.

Behind them came the pick-and-shovel crew—filling the stump holes from "borrow pits" along the side of the road, breaking stones, clearing the small mesquite bushes and the yellow-blazing patches of brittlebush, raking them over to the bonfires.

The scraper came next—two timbers bolted together and pulled by a wagon team. Six men, Manring one of them, stood on the timbers to add weight. The scraper bumped along over the roadway, the convicts losing their balance, jumping off and on, and every ten or fifteen feet the team was pulled off to the side, dragging with it the loose rocks and sand that the timbers gathered.

Two men with shovels came last—filling the potholes that the scraper passed over and did not fill completely. Renda stayed even with them, walking his horse along the east-wall shade approximately one hundred feet behind Brazil.

The Mimbreños were up on the canyon patrolling along both sides. They remained in the shadows of the pinyon pines and were not seen all morning, not until Renda stopped work at noon.

As the convicts drifted over to the east wall where the equipment wagon stood, Salvaje and two of his Mimbres came down a shallow wash, a dust cloud trailing behind them. They were riding past the equipment wagon when Renda called to them and they pulled up. The two Mimbres sat their horses, motionlessly watching Salvaje rein toward Renda who was now facing the convicts grouped at the back end of the equipment wagon. He pointed to Bowen, Pryde and the Mexican. "You three step out," he called. Then turned to Salvaje again. "You're going to the creek?"

The Mimbreño nodded and held up three fingers. "That many at a time."

"Take these men with you," Renda said. "They're going to water the teams."

The Mimbres moved off one at a time as each pair of horses was brought out. Salvaje waited until Bowen came up, then fell in next to him and they moved the team down canyon, winding through the scattered scrub brush to a stand of sycamores that showed darkly against the west slope. A trickle of water came down from the rocks and formed a shallow pool in the deep shade of the trees. From here, the creek flowed to the end of the canyon, disappeared into the rocks and came out again miles to the south, above the Pinaleño station.

They drank: the convicts first, the Mimbres one at a time, and now they rested as the horses stood over the clear, sand-bottomed pool, their muzzles touching the water, rippling the water with breath from their nostrils, raising and shaking their manes, tails fanning lazily and now and again a rump or flank quivering to dislodge an unseen something.

Salvaje touched Bowen's arm. "But for the work of getting more horses, I wish you would run away another time."

Bowen frowned. "I don't understand."

"That was a good thing with you in the meadow," Salvaje explained. "But the two horses you killed I was made to replace."

"Renda made you buy two horses?"

Salvaje shrugged. "Not buy; but it is the same thing."

"You'd think he'd supply the horses," Bowen said.

Salvaje shook his head. "He is not easy to live with. Sometimes I see him as an escaped man. If he was ever that, he would not be brought back alive."

Bowen hesitated. The Mimbre's words took him by surprise and stayed in his mind as he said, "You speak English very well."

"From San Carlos."

"I visited Cibucu many times," Bowen said. "When I was trading horses. I knew Zele and Pindah and Bu-sikisn."

Salvaje's eyes came alive. "They were of Victorio."

Bowen nodded. "I drank tulapai with Zele and he told me much about Victorio and old Mangas."

"Perhaps I was there then," Salvaje said.

"They spoke of a band still in the Sierra Madres," Bowen said. "Maybe you were there."

Salvaje nodded thoughtfully. "The good days. At San Carlos it was not easy to live among Tontos and Mojaves."

"But better than here?" Bowen asked.

"Sometimes. The men such as you make it worth staying here."

"The men who run?"

"The ones who know how to run. Some are like children about it. Others do well."

"Listen," Bowen said then, "I'm sorry I cracked a couple of heads that day. I mean that truthfully, because I don't have any fight with you or your men."

Salvaje's eyes held on Bowen and he studied him thoughtfully, as if wanting to understand all of Bowen, all of the things about him that would never be spoken. Finally he said, "Maybe you try it again some time."

Bowen nodded. "Maybe I will."

The team horses raised their heads from the pool a moment before Bowen heard the leaf-rustling, twig-snapping sound of someone coming through the trees. He looked up as Salvaje rose, expecting to see another of the Mimbres or one of the guards and his face showed open surprise as Karla Demery walked her horse into the clearing.

Bowen saw her look directly at him, then her skirt curved gracefully as she stepped from the saddle. Again, she was wearing a man's shirt and her dark hair was even shorter than he had pictured it—curving low on her forehead, but brushed back on the sides into a soft upcurl at the nape of her neck. And Bowen was thinking, watching her take her horse to the pool edge: I'll bet she can ride like hell. I'll bet she can cook and shoot and do everything like hell. But, he thought then, seeing her looking at him again and feeling the sudden quickening inside of him: Don't try to figure her out.

Karla's gaze moved from Bowen and Salvaje to Pryde and the Mexican, then raised to the two Mimbres standing behind them. To no one in particular she said, "No guards? I'm surprised at Mr. Renda."

Squatting at the edge of the pool, the Mexican pushed up his hatbrim with his thumb. "These barbarians are guards enough."

"I'm still surprised," Karla said. Her eyes returned to Bowen and Salvaje. "I'm delivering mail to the camp, but I might as well leave it with you." She looked directly at Bowen. "You'll see that Mr. Renda gets it?"

Bowen nodded. "Sure." He started to rise and Salvaje stepped in front of him.

"Your friend understands English?" Karla said.

Bowen glanced at Salvaje. "Very well."

Karla was looking at the Mimbre now. "I'll give it to this man—Bowen."

Salvaje shook his head.

"We're missing two horses," Karla said evenly. "Both of them wearing a Double-H brand. Would you like the San Carlos man to visit your ranchería?"

The Mimbre stared at her, not answering.

"Mr. Bowen," Karla said. "You'll find the mail in the left-hand saddlebag."

Bowen hesitated. He walked around the pool then, past the team horses, feeling Salvaje and the others watching him. He saw Karla leaning close to the horse patting its neck, but as he came around to its off side she straightened up and moved toward him.

"Let me help you."

"What're you up to?"

Close to him she began unbuckling the flap of the saddle bag. "Just listen to me."

"They can hear us!"

"Then don't talk!" Her voice dropped to a half-whisper as she said, "I heard from the lawyer in Prescott. He's agreed to look into your trial, but he wants a few things cleared up."

Bowen frowned. "Why should he help me?"

"Because I asked him to!"

"He can't—"

"Be quiet and listen!" She spoke rapidly then, her voice a soft, hoarse whisper. "Think back and don't waste words when I ask you a question, Mr. Martz says there's little mention of the bill of sale in the court records. Was it shown as evidence?"

"It was shown for a minute."

"Did Manring admit forging Mr. McLaughlin's signature?"

"That didn't come up."

"But it was a copy of McLaughlin's style of writing."

"I think so."

"Then why didn't they try to find out who filled out and signed the bill of sale?"

"The judge assumed it was Manring."

"How would Manring know how McLaughlin wrote?"

"McLaughlin claimed Earl worked for him three years before."

"And he'd remember McLaughlin's script?"

Bowen hesitated. "Wait a minute. You're assuming Earl forged the receipt . . . that he stole the cattle!"

"Mr. Martz is assuming it. He knows McLaughlin well, a man with a good reputation. He's never done anything like this in his life. He's never had to. With the land he has, taking a few hundred dollars from Manring wouldn't be worth the bother."

"If Earl forged the receipt, I don't know how he did it."

"Neither does Mr. Martz. That's the first thing he has to find out. Next...was the bill of sale made out on plain paper?"

"No, it had McLaughlin's letterhead on it."

"His regular stock-sale receipt?"

"That's what it looked like."

"Where did Manring get it?"

"All I know is what he told me. McLaughlin gave it to him."

"Which isn't true."

"Your lawyer friend's doing a lot of assuming."

"It's his business. This isn't something new to him."

"He's sure about McLaughlin?"

"Of course he's sure! He's lived in Prescott for twenty years and has known Mr. McLaughlin longer than that." Karla pulled a bundle of letters from the saddle bag and pushed it at Bowen. "Manring couldn't have known enough about McLaughlin's handwriting to copy the signature himself. He wasn't in a position to pick up a blank bill of sale form. So...who did?"

"Maybe I'd better ask Earl."

Karla shook her head. "Don't do anything until I hear from Mr. Martz again."

"There's not a lot I *can* do."

"Talking to Manring could lead to a fight."

"That might be all right."

"That would be fine. You'd end up out of reach in the punishment cell. What if Mr. Martz wanted information from you?"

"All right."

"Don't do *anything!*" Karla turned from him. She picked up her reins, mounted and rode into the trees without looking back.

Pryde, sitting next to the Mexican at the edge of the pool, watched Bowen come back toward them. He saw him hand the bundle of letters to Salvaje who took them but said nothing.

"Corey, you know that girl very long?"

Bowen looked down at Pryde. "I guess long enough."

The Mexican shook his head, grinning. "Too bad we couldn't hear."

When they returned with the team horses, Bowen watched Salvaje ride over to Renda and hand him the mail. They spoke for less than a minute and, watching Salvaje ride off, Bowen was sure he had not told Renda about it. They had not talked long enough.

His spirits rose. He ate his jerky and pan bread, drank the lukewarm coffee and thought about Karla Demery: picturing her, going over and over again in his mind what she had said; then projecting from there: seeing her again, this time telling him the lawyer had found something, *something,* whatever it was, that proved his innocence; then later, on an evening, Karla and the lawyer—Martz? —riding into the convict camp, the lawyer handing Renda a signed release and Renda standing, taking it, reading it with his mouth open.

Hit him then, Bowen thought.

No, you can't have everything.

And don't count on it, he thought then. What is the *something* the lawyer finds? The odds are against your getting out of here. Even with an A-1 Prescott Hatch & Hodges lawyer...and Karla Demery.

But even as he told himself this, his hopes were up and he went back to work almost eagerly—and with something of a feeling that he should be working harder since Karla and the lawyer were doing so much to get him out.

Pryde said nothing more to him about the girl. But after they had pulled out the first pinyon stump and the Mexican was dragging it off to the fire, Chick Miller said, "I hear you got a sweetheart." He looked at Bowen slyly, one eye almost closed beneath the cocked brim of his straw hat.

"Is that what you hear, Chick?"

"From a little bird," Chick said, grinning.

"From a little Mex bird," Pryde said.

Chick looked at him as if surprised. "What, it's supposed to be a secret? You can't stand talking close to a girl in broad daylight and expect it to be a secret."

"She was giving me the mail," Bowen said.

"To *you,* not to the Indin."

"Maybe she's the kind," Pryde said, "who figures you can't trust a 'Pache."

"Sure," Chick nodded, grinning again. "Corey, you must've known her before."

"She was giving me the mail," Bowen said again.

Chick winked at him. "I'd let her give me the mail anytime."

"Be careful now."

"I didn't mean any offense."

They moved on to the next stump and when the Mexican returned Pryde said, "You talk a hell of a lot."

"Me?"

"You know what I'm talking about."

"I told that the girl spoke to Bowen," the Mexican said. "What about it?"

"He didn't tell me what was said." Chick shook his head. "Not one word."

"Because I didn't hear," the Mexican said. "I didn't hear anything they were saying."

"Let's drop it there," Bowen said. He looked from Pryde to Chick to the Mexican. "All right?"

"Well," Chick said, "if it's something you're ashamed of. Though she doesn't look like a girl you'd be ashamed to be seen talking to."

Over Chick's shoulder, Pryde saw Brazil coming toward them. He had left his horse close to the canyon wall, although there was no shade there now with the sun directly overhead, and was walking toward them, carrying the Winchester under his arm.

"You better shut your mouth," Pryde told Chick.

Chick turned on him unexpectedly. "Who in hell you think you are? You're no better than anybody else! You think—"

"You better shut up." Pryde saw Brazil coming up behind Chick.

"Why, because you say so?" Chick placed his hands on his hips defiantly. "I don't have to take anything from you or anybody like you! It's enough to have to stomach Renda and Brazil telling you what to do!" Chick paused. "One more year and I'm out of here and they're going to pay. Sure as there's a God upstairs they're going to pay for every last dirty thing they've done to me."

"You're sure about that?"

Chick did not move. Pryde saw the shocked surprise,

then fear come over his face—his eyes wide and his mouth open as if to cry out. Then, with an effort, with a lip-biting jaw-tensed effort, his expression slowly changed and his face was almost relaxed as he turned to Brazil.

"What're you going to do to me?"

"What do you think?" Brazil asked mildly.

"I don't want to get hit."

"I'll bet you don't."

"Listen"—Chick swallowed and the fear was in his eyes again—"I was just talking. You know how you get mad and say funny things—"

"I didn't think it was funny."

"Not *funny*. You know, you say things you don't mean."

"The first thing that comes into your mind."

"That's right. No! Wild, crazy things that you don't mean, but just so you'll be saying something."

"Like making me pay."

Chick tried to smile. "That's right. How could I make you pay? See what I mean, that's just crazy talk that came in my head."

Brazil raised the Winchester, holding it across his chest. "And you don't think I ought to hit you?"

Chick swallowed again. He started to back away. "Beating me wouldn't solve anything."

"Maybe it wouldn't at that," Brazil said. He lowered the Winchester so that the stock was beneath his right arm, his right hand gripped through the lever. He moved toward Chick who half turned and began edging away.

"What are you going to do?"

"Run down and tell Renda to come here," Brazil said.

"You mean it?"

"I wouldn't say it 'less I did."

"You're not going to do anything to me?"

"Go on."

Chick edged away, still half turned looking at Brazil. He glanced up canyon to locate Renda, looked back at Brazil once more then turned, his quick short steps developing into a run. He had gone no more than thirty feet when Brazil fired. Chick stumbled as if trying to turn and Brazil fired again, the stock of the Winchester still under his arm and held just above his waist. He levered another shell into the chamber before his gaze returned from Chick Miller to the three men near him. His eyes moved slowly from Bowen to Pryde to the Mexican.

"He tried to run," Brazil said. "You saw him. He tried to run away."

EIGHT

RENDA made them remove Chick Miller's clothes before burying him. Bowen and Pryde took turns digging a grave close to the canyon slope; then, after they had lowered Chick's body into it and pushed in the dirt, the Mexican covered the low mound with stones and marked the grave with a cross he had made by tying together two mesquite sticks with a length of pinyon root.

"He never learned to keep his mouth shut," Pryde said. They were walking back to the team now, the Mexican ahead of them dragging the chain to the next stump.

"There wasn't any sense to it," Bowen said. "I saw him do it, but if I hadn't, I wouldn't believe it. You don't just kill a man like that—like you don't have anything better to do."

"Now you know what kind Brazil is," Pryde said.

"It's hard to believe," Bowen said. "A man with only a year left and he had to say the wrong thing."

"I wonder," Pryde said, "if Renda will write to his wife."

"He's got a family?"

"Sure, a wife and two girls in Wickenburg."

Bowen shook his head. "If he could've held out just one more year, maybe he could've made them pay. Like he said."

"That was talk," Pryde said. "By the time you get out Renda'll be in some other business. Even if he's still working convicts, how're you going to prove anything?"

"I was thinking—maybe twist Willis Falvey's arm."

"If you can get to him."

"Renda'll have Willis write the letter," Bowen said.

"Which is about all Willis's good for."

"Ike . . . do you have a family?"

"I wouldn't be here if I did."

Bowen said, "Something like that can't happen too many times. All of a sudden every convict here will start swinging picks and shovels. There's only so much a man can take. They'll say it's better to get killed with a chance of

67

escaping than getting cut down for saying the wrong thing . . . Ike, what if all of a sudden the thirty of us rushed them? Thirty against four."

"Thirty against three Winchesters and a scatter gun," Pryde said.

"But if it was timed right—"

"And if the Mimbres were on our side."

"Let's take one thing at a time."

"It's all at the same time," Pryde said. "Soon as one shot is fired the Mimbres are aiming down the slopes, on both sides."

But it's got to be done somehow. Bowen thought. And soon. You keep still so long then one day you say the wrong thing and Brazil says, "Go get Renda." He could say anything. "Go over and get that shovel," or he could pull the trigger right in front of you. What difference would it make? Nobody's bringing him to court for it. In the records it's still *killed while trying to escape*. Picture six years of pulling stumps and trying not to say the wrong thing. Six years of Renda . . . and Brazil. After this camp, some other one, and if not Renda and Brazil, men just like them, because you don't get the love-thy-neighbor kind to boss convicts. Or else you go back to Yuma . . . to the granite cells and the desert and the Gatling gun over the main gate.

And if not six years, he thought picturing Karla, then how long? A year? Two years? How long do you think it'll take that lawyer—assuming he'll get you freed? Longer than you could stand. She's some girl and it would be fine to know her better, but it even takes a week to get a letter from Prescott. So add up how many letters and how many weeks. Can you stand it even that long, a week? Maybe. But you have to be looking forward to something to do it.

Cross the lawyer off, Bowen thought. Cross off everything that isn't certain or anything that's more than a week away. Then concentrate on one thing. She's some girl, he thought then, but it would've been better if she gave you a gun instead of a lawyer.

Renda stopped work at six o'clock. The convicts filed past the equipment wagon to drop shovels, picks and axes, then boarded the two wagons that waited behind. Bowen hitched the team to the third wagon. He walked back to the end gate then to climb on and as he did, Earl Manring held our his hand to help him.

"That was too bad," Manring said, "about Chick."

The wagons strained over the uneven ground, were pulled in a wide slow turn and started back up canyon to the wash they had come down that morning. Bowen moved with the swaying, jolting motion of the wagon, his eyes on Renda and Brazil again bringing up the rear.

"I said that was too bad about Chick," Manring repeated.

"I heard you."

"Don't you think it was?"

"Earl, if you have something to say, say it."

Manring grinned. "I hear you got a sweetheart."

Bowen turned to him. "That's the way Chick started. He went right on talking till the end."

"That was too bad about Chick," Manring said thoughtfully. "Something that could happen to anybody. Right?"

Bowen shrugged.

"Corey, I got something to talk over with you." Manring leaned closer to him to say it.

"What about?"

"Later on tonight we'll talk about it."

"Then what'd you bring it up for?"

"To see if you were still as agreeable as ever," Manring grinned.

The last red reflection of the sun showed in the sky behind them as the wagons rolled down the slope toward the camp—toward the silent, cold-looking, deserted-looking adobes that were already enveloped in the dull shadow of this slope the wagons were descending.

Now, at the gate, a lantern flickered, then went up to full brightness. Minutes later, off to the right of the gate, another light appeared showing the black square of the stable entrance. As the wagons neared the gate, a third lantern blinked on, this one to the left. It hung from the ramada in front of Renda's quarters, and now a shadowy figure could be seen standing close to one of the support posts.

One of the night guards turned the corner of the convicts' barracks as the wagons pulled up. He struck a match to light the lantern that hung head-high next to the middle door, then leaned against the wall, the match stick in the corner of his mouth, and watched the convicts unload.

When they were lined up he counted them. Then counted them again before looking at Renda.

"You're one short."

"We're supposed to be," Renda answered. "Feed 'em and put 'em to bed." He turned away, walking across the yard toward the lantern that hung from the ramada. In the dimness a figure waited for him, then stepped into the light as Renda approached the adobe.

"I heard what that guard said."

Renda looked up. "Then you got good ears, Willis."

"You let somebody escape, didn't you?"

"I didn't let anybody escape."

"Damn it, the guard said you were short one!"

"Willis, we buried a man today. That's why we're short."

"What happened?"

"What do you think? He tried to run. Brazil shot him."

Falvey exhaled slowly. "What if he'd made it?"

"Nobody has yet,' Renda answered.

"But what if he had?"

"What if you stop worrying about it?"

"Frank, if a man got out and told what's going on here—"

"Who'd listen to him? It'd be your word against his."

Falvey shook his head. "We can't take a chance on even the possibility of it."

"Willis, nobody's ever escaped from me and nobody's going to."

"Those men are thinking about it all the time."

"Let them. Thinking about it and doing it are about seven hundred miles apart."

"But sooner or later—"

Renda shook his head. "Not sooner or later or any time. I'll talk to them, Willis. All I got to do is talk to them."

After the evening meal, the convicts were marched to the stock tank in back of the stable—a round, waist-high tin-lined tank fed by a thin but steady flow of water that emptied from a rusted pipe connected to the well shaft of the windmill.

They were given fifteen minutes to wash as much of themselves as they cared to, and shave if they wanted to do that. Part of a mirror was fastened to a timber of the wind-mill structure and above it a lantern hung from a nail. One mirror, four dull razors and a few chunks of soap for thirty men. For that reason few of the men shaved more than twice a week and almost a third of them wore beards. For them, Renda produced a pair of scissors once a week.

Most of the convicts removed only their shirts, splashed water over their faces and upper bodies to remove twelve hours of grime and sweat, then dried themselves with the shirts before putting them on again.

After that, they were marched back to the barracks, counted again, then moved inside. The three lanterns that hung from wires hooked to the ceiling would burn for an hour and a half. At the end of that time, a night guard would come in for a last check and order the lanterns out.

But this night did not follow the usual routine.

Shortly before nine o'clock, one of the gaurds came in. Two of the convicts rose from their mats to put out the lanterns.

"Keep them on!"

They looked at the guard. Then every man in the room looked at him and a silence followed. They watched him glance over his shoulder then step aside as Renda came in, his shotgun under his arm, followed by Brazil and the two day guards who were all carrying Winchesters. Brazil stopped near Renda, but the two guards moved past him to cover the convicts nearer the end of the room.

Renda waited and his eyes moved slowly over the convicts. Most of them were on their own mats now, but a few of them here and there were still grouped together over a card game. Renda waited until he was sure they were all looking toward him, until there was not the smallest foot-scuffing sound.

Then he began: "Chick Miller got killed today," Renda stated. "He was trying to escape. Brazil warned him—called out for Chick to halt, but Chick kept going, so he didn't have any choice but to shoot him. That's what happened, so that's what the official report will say that goes to Prescott," Renda paused. "Does anybody say it happened any different?"

No one spoke. Renda's eyes moved along the line of men, then stopped at Bowen. "Stand up."

Bowen pushed himself up, turned to face Renda.

Renda's eyes held on him. "Isn't that how it happened?"

Calmly, quietly, Bowen said, "If you say so, then that's how it happened."

"Chick tried to run and Brazil had to shoot him," Renda stated.

Bowen nodded. "All right."

"Sit down." Renda's eyes moved to Pryde, then to the Mexican. He asked them the same question and both of them agreed that it had happened as Renda said it did.

"Now I'll tell you something," Renda said, including all the convicts. "Nobody here's going to ever try that again. I'm giving orders to shoot, the least move out of line. You hesitate one second when you're told to do something, you're dead. You take one step in the wrong direction and you won't know what hit you. I want you to understand that. I want you to get it in your heads so clear you won't move without thinking about it." He turned to Bowen suddenly. "You understand that?"

Bowen nodded, looking up at Renda.

"You understand it," Renda said. "You were standing close to Chick. Listen, I'll tell you something else. That stunt you pulled a while back . . . jumping off the wagon. You wouldn't get just twenty days for it the second time."

He looked over all the convicts. "You get past the guards, the Mimbres have got orders to take your scalp. You won't be brought back here . . . just part of you. To prove you're dead.

"I'm giving you warning now," Renda continued. "One move out of line and somebody shoots. You'll even think before spitting over the side of the wagon. What you're doing to get shot don't matter to me. It goes in the report as trying to escape and the report's the only thing that means anything. So you think about that."

Again his gaze moved slowly over the convicts, then he turned and left the barracks. Brazil and the guards followed him, the last one giving the order for the lanterns to be put out. Outside, they heard the lock snap on the door, the sound of footsteps fading away, then silence.

Moments later, something touched Bowen's foot. He sat up quietly.

"Who is it?"

"Come over here."

He recognized Earl Manring's voice. As he rose, Manring moved away. A moment later he saw Manring's outline against the window that was almost directly across from him. It was early and there was little moonlight, but enough to show the narrow shape of the window. Half of the opening had been boarded up from the outside, the other half covered by a heavy-gauge wire screen.

As Bowen reached him, Manring asked, "He scare you?"

Bowen's hand touched the window sill. "He gave you something to think about."

"That's all talk."

"You didn't see Chick get shot."

"Brazil didn't like Chick. He never did. That's why he killed him."

"Brazil doesn't like anybody."

Manring shook his head. "If you don't make any noise, you don't get in any trouble. Chick was always talking. Brazil got to the point he couldn't stand it any more. He might've thought he was even doing everybody a favor shooting him."

"That's a nice thought," Bowen said.

"You're in the same spot as Chick," Manring went on. "They're watching you because you tried to run one time. I told you it wasn't the right time, but you wouldn't listen to me . . . Corey, they're no meaner than they ever were. They'll shoot anybody they don't like . . . let you alone if you don't make trouble."

"You're one of the good ones, Earl?"

"One of the smart ones if you want to get down to it. I didn't spend no twenty days in the hole."

"You were out working."

"And looking around," Manring said.

"Go on."

"You're still thinking about it . . . after what Renda said?"

"Frank makes you want to get out all the more."

"I've got to be sure of you," Manring said.

"As sure as I am of you?"

Manring's eyes narrowed. "What's that supposed to mean?"

"You think about it a while."

"Look," Manring said. "I don't have to include you. If you're going to start accusing me again we'll forget about it. I'll get somebody else."

"Earl, the only reason you're asking anybody is because getting out of here is something you can't do alone. I'm not sure yet why you're picking me. Maybe because you thought I was easy to manage before. Whatever the reason, it's something that'll do you the most good."

73

Manring shrugged. "Forget about it then."

"I can, Earl, but you can't. I just told you why."

"You're pretty sure of yourself."

Bowen started to turn away.

"Wait a minute—" Manring's hand came out to take his arm. "Listen, there's no sense in arguing over it. Let's get down to cases ... you either want to go or you don't. Which is it?"

"I haven't heard any plan yet," Bowen said.

"That'll come."

"It'll come right now, or I don't."

"I'll tell you part of it," Manring paused. Then, his voice was lower as he said, "You know what happens at the end of the canyon."

"We climb," Bowen said.

"That's right. Have you figured how we're going to cut a road up through the rocks?"

"It isn't my problem."

"It wasn't mine either," Manring said, "till I was taken on Renda's survey party. That was over a month ago ... when we planned this swing through the canyon. We got up to the end and he says, 'How in hell we going to get out of here?' Right then is when the idea came. I said to him, 'What're you worrying about those big rocks for when you got a gang of Yuma boys on your payroll?' He stopped to listen and I told him how at Yuma we cut whole cell blocks out of granite and shaped them just right. He thought about it and then says, 'You're making work for yourself, aren't you?' That's when I told him. I said, 'Well, it's not so bad if you got dynamite.' "

"So he's going to use it?" Bowen prompted.

"It's already ordered," Manring said. "Should be here by next week."

"Earl, are you going to tell me you talked him into using dynamite?"

"I put the idea in his head. You can call it whatever you want."

"You think," Bowen said, "he would've plotted down that canyon without planning on dynamite?"

"Renda don't know anything about road building!"

Bowen paused. "Let me ask you something else, Earl. Do you know how to use dynamite?"

"I saw enough of it at Yuma."

"That's right, you *saw* it...but there's only one man here you're sure ever worked with it. That's where I figure in. You've got the plan, but you need me to set it off."

"You're taking on a lot of credit all of a sudden," Manring muttered. "Next you'll tell me you were planning on it all the time."

"No," Bowen admitted. "I never thought of breaking out of here as being worth blowing somebody up."

"Well, think about it now," Manring said quietly. "Think about this afternoon, the way that gunhand busted Chick Miller...think about them watching you, looking for the littlest excuse to bust you...and let me know what you come to."

That same evening, Lizann Falvey learned from her husband that a convict had been killed. She thought of Bowen, and for some time was very sure that he was dead. Willis did not know the convict's name. He knew only what Renda had told him—that a convict had tried to run away and Brazil had no choice but to shoot him. By then, the convicts were locked in the barracks for the night and Lizann had no way of finding out whether or not the man had been Bowen.

She considered asking Renda directly, but almost immediately decided against it. Her interest in Bowen could arouse Renda's suspicion and she could not risk any word or action which might do that. Not now. Not with the plan that would enable her to leave here already in her mind. She had thought it out carefully and deliberately. It was the simplest way, as far as Lizann's part in it was concerned, and it offered the least chance of error. Still, the decision to carry out the plan remained with Bowen.

The next morning Lizann was up before six o'clock and standing at the window as the wagons made their slow turn coming away from the barracks. There. Bowen was in the third wagon. She watched him until the wagon passed through the gate, relieved now in knowing she would not have to go to the trouble of—as she heard it in her own mind—breaking in a new man. Now her only problem was to get Bowen alone.

The opportunity came the next Sunday. It came unexpectedly and Lizann was almost unprepared for it.

Willis had left for Fuegos by midmorning. For almost an

hour after that Lizann gazed out of the window watching the convicts standing along the front of the barracks. Bowen was among them. Bowen, and next to him, the man who had been with him in the punishment cell.

He could be sent to the stable again, Lizann thought. She went into the bedroom and changed to her riding suit, but when she returned, Bowen was still there.

Be patient, she thought. But even while thinking this she decided to take her horse out.

Frank Renda closed his door behind him as Lizann stepped outside.

"Going for a ride?" Renda asked.

How do you answer a question like that? Lizann thought and decided not to answer it at all. She started across the compound and Renda fell in next to her.

"You're not very sociable today."

"Is today different from any other?"

"It's Sunday. The day of rest...Rest for most." Renda was looking toward the convicts. His eyes found Bowen and Pryde and he called out to them. As they came toward him Renda said, "But no rest for these two."

"The stable?" Pryde asked.

"What'd you think?" Renda said. "That's your permanent Sunday job."

Inside the stable, Lizann watched Pryde pick up a broom and walk down to the far end. She heard Renda say to Bowen, "Saddle up my chestnut."

As he moved to Renda's stall, Lizann said, "Ask him to saddle mine, too."

Renda glanced at her. "You like to be waited on, don't you?"

"No more than you do," Lizann answered.

Renda shrugged, looking at Bowen then. "Do what she says."

Now—Lizann thought.

"Frank," she said, turning to leave the stable. "Have him bring it over to me...I've forgotten something."

She walked out, not waiting to hear Renda's answer, then took her time crossing the yard, glancing indifferently from the convicts to the guard at the main gate. She entered her adobe, leaving the door open, then hurried into the bedroom. From the top drawer of the dresser, she took the .25-caliber Colt revolver and returned with it to the front room. As she did, looking out through the open door and across the wide expanse of yard, she saw Renda ride out of the stable toward the gate. A few minutes later Bowen came out leading her sorrel.

Lizann smiled and she was thinking: Frank, if you knew how easy you were making it.

She remained back out of the doorway, now holding the revolver at her side, hidden in the folds of her full riding skirt. Bowen approached the ramada, then halted at the edge of the shade. He could not yet see her, but he called out, "Here's your horse."

Lizann answered, "Come inside."

Bowen hesitated. He glanced toward the barracks, then let the reins fall and entered the adobe. He nodded, seeing Lizann. "You worked that good."

"Thank you." Lizann smiled momentarily. "Where is Frank going?"

"He didn't say."

"He made it very easy for us."

"I can still get caught in here. Brazil's about."

Lizann moved toward him. "I heard a man was killed the other day and I thought it was you. I was almost sure it was."

"If it was," Bowen said, "you'd have to break in a new man."

Lizann hesitated. "I'm never quite sure what you're going to say."

"It's true, isn't it?"

She moved closer to him and put her hand on his arm. "I was thinking of you, Corey. Not just a man who's willing to help me."

Bowen said nothing.

Lizann's eyebrows raised. "What happened to our beautiful friendship?"

"It's as beautiful as it ever was."

"Do you still want to help me?"

"If it means helping myself."

Lizann gazed up at him, studying his face. "You seem farther away, Corey. Do you feel I'm not acting like a lady?"

"I haven't been picturing you as one."

She dropped her eyes. "I was, once. Before I was brought here."

Come on, Bowen thought. Get to the point.

"It isn't just Renda and having to live here like a prisoner—which is more than any woman should be asked to bear. It's also my husband."

"We've been over your husband before."

"I thought you were more understanding."

"I'm trying to understand one thing—why you brought me in here."

Her eyes lowered again. "If you really knew what kind of a man my husband is... The way he treats me—"

"Look," Bowen said patiently. "I'm convinced. Let's get to the point."

She looked at him calmly now, without pretense. "You don't think very highly of me, do you?"

"It wouldn't matter one way or the other," Bowen said. "Do you have something, or don't you?"

Lizann's hand came out of the folds of her skirt and she pressed the barrel of the revolver against Bowen's belt buckle. "I have this," she said and caught the momentary surprise in Bowen's eyes as he saw the revolver. "Will it help?"

Bowen nodded slowly, thoughtfully. "It'll help."

"Then it's yours," Lizann said. "On one condition."

Bowen's hand went to the revolver. The short barrel remained pressed against him and he could feel her finger on the trigger. "What's the condition?"

"How you escape from here is your business," Lizann said. "You can have the gun and use it however you like. That will be no concern of mine. I'm not asking you to take me with you."

"What's the condition?" Bowen asked again.

"That you kill my husband first," Lizann said calmly.

NINE

THE SECOND LETTER from Lyall Martz, the Hatch & Hodges attorney, arrived on the Saturday afternoon stage. It came unexpectedly, for Karla had written to him only the day after talking to Bowen, Tuesday, and there had not been time for her letter even to reach Prescott, much less receive an answer already.

Her father watched her. "Well, go ahead and read it."

"I'm afraid to," Karla said.

"You're not going to change what's inside by staring at the envelope."

"It's bad news," Karla said tonelessly. "Either he's decided not to work on it or else he's run up against a stone wall."

"Sis, that's some gift you have—being able to read letters without opening them."

She glanced at her father. "It has to be one or the other. Mr. Martz hasn't even received my letter yet. He couldn't have been working on it—he needed the information he asked for first."

"Then," Demery said, "he couldn't have run into a stone wall...not yet."

Karla nodded dejectedly. "He's decided he can't spare the time. That must be it."

"Sis, if you don't hurry up and read it, I'll have to."

"I will," Karla said.

Demery watched her finger work open the envelope, take out the letter and unfold the pages bearing Lyall Martz's large, down-slanting scrawl. He watched her—a frown, a somber tight-lipped expression on her face, now biting her lower lip lightly, thoughtfully, now her lips parting and not biting them, her eyes opening, opening wide, glancing up, but only for part of a moment, concentrating on the letter again, and her mouth began to form a smile. She looked up again and the smile was in her eyes: a moist, glistening smile that struck John Demery as the most genuinely happy smile he had ever seen in his life.

"Bad news?"

Karla's lips moved, but no sound came from them.

"Are you going to read it to me," Demery said, "or do I have to guess."

She stared at him, still smiling, and handed him the letter. "Read it out loud."

"This must be some letter,' Demery said. He began to read:

Dear Karla,

As soon as I accepted this "spare-time job" as you call it, I had to admit to a weakening of the will. I am afraid my giving in has touched off a complete breakdown of my mental faculties, for now I must admit to even a weakening in the intellect department. (Don't tell your father that, though he wouldn't understand it anyway.)

Demery looked up, but before he could speak Karla said, "Go one, read."

After I wrote to you [Demery continued] outlining the information I needed, it occurred to me: how is Karla going to get information from a man locked up in a convict camp? That could be difficult even for Karla. Then I realized that all I need do was talk to McLaughlin myself. He was at the trial and, of course, he saw the bill of sale. Which I did.

Mac stated that the handwriting on the bill of sale was clearly an imitation of his own, and a fairly good one, especially the signature. My reasoning then eliminated both your friend Bowen and the other one, Manring, as the forger. It is possible that they know how to write but highly improbable they write well enough to copy the ornate signature McLaughlin has been practicing for fifty years.

That pointed to a third man. I asked Mac if the identity of the forger was established at the trial. He recalled that it had not even been brought up. He also told me that Manring had worked for him once before, though had denied it at the trial. Could Manring have procured a blank bill of sale at that time? Yes, but that had been three years ago, Mac stated. Only six months before the trial, he had purchased new stationery and forms. The bill of sale was of the new batch.

Now, so far we have established that there must be a third man. But, who?

Probably anyone who worked for McLaughlin could have come by a blank bill of sale. He admitted that. But again, we eliminated three-quarters of his hands on the basis of not being able to write at all. So it must be a man who wrote well enough himself to copy another so exactly. Still, a man who worked for McLaughlin.

His bookkeeper? No, Mac said. He kept his own books since firing Roy Avery. McLaughlin looked at me and I looked at him and that, Karla, was how it happened. You see, McLaughlin always tended his own paper work until deciding a man of his holdings should have a bookkeeper of his own. (It took him twenty years to decide this.) So he hired Avery, who lasted two months. He did nothing dishonest, then. But Mac didn't care for him in general and when he fired him they had an argument over the justice of it.

If the identity of the forger had been investigated at the trial, Mr. Avery's name would already appear in the record. That is how obvious it was his doing. Being obvious, Roy Avery of course left Prescott at the time the two men were apprehended. But—and it is questionable whether this is evidence of nerve or imbecility— Mr. Avery returned to Prescott upon learning there had been no mention of him made at the trial. Hence, he was arrested right here in Prescott, McLaughlin having agreed to proffer charges.

Yesterday morning Roy Avery signed a statement admitting his part in the case. He stated that his dealings were with Earl Manring only, that he had never met a Corey Bowen, had never even heard of him until the trial.

As far as he knew, Manring had planned to take the cattle alone. If Bowen helped him, Avery stated, then he was fairly certain Bowen was working at what he believed to be an honest job. Avery reasoned it this way: if Bowen knew it was rustled stock, he would have demanded a close to equal share in the profit. Knowing Manring, Avery said, Manring would never have agreed to that. Therefore, since Bowen *did* go along, Avery believes he was drawing nothing more than trail wages. We must compliment Mr. Avery on a piece of uncommonly sound reasoning.

This morning, Karla, I filed a motion for a new trial. The date has not yet been set, but I think your friend has a much better than average chance of winning an acquittal. And I generally do not make predictions.

Incidentally, the court record stated that neither of the two men had been arrested previously. However that meant only that the Prescott sheriff's office did not have a wanted dodger on either of them. Tracing Manring's past seemed almost impossible to begin with and after a wire to the Tucson authorities, and receiving a negative reply, I gave up on him. However I was able to find out something about Bowen.

His last job was with a cattle company headquartered in the San Rafael valley. But before that he seemed to have spent most of his time in mining. His record showed his first job had been with the Moctezuma people in Bisbee. I wired them and found out he had lived there most of his life. His father had been a mine foreman with Moctezuma and Bowen worked for him on and off, sometimes going up into the hills alone to try his own luck, until the father was killed in a mine shaft cave-in. Shortly after that, Bowen left Bisbee. He worked for a horse trader about two years then joined the San Rafael cattle outfit. His mother had passed away some time before the father and as far as I can discover, your friend has no other kin in the territory.

Girl, if all this sounds overly quick and simple, put it out of your head. I have been working harder at my "spare time job" than at my regular practice or for Hatch and Hodges. It is fortunate, Karla, that you have a pretty face (even if your father does claim you are half boy), or you never would have talked me into this.

I expect to be in Willcox some time next month and look forward to seeing your mother and sisters. If I have time, I will stop by Pinaleño on the way back.

> With love,
> Your UNCLE LYALL

"Your Uncle Lyall," Demery repeated, looking up at Karla. "I hope he isn't claiming kinship from my side of the family."

Karla was still smiling. "And you said he'd be wasting his time."

"He hasn't *proved* anything, Karla."

"He has for me."

"And now you'll want to go up and tell your friend about it."

"I have to take the mail anyway."

"Not today, you won't. It'd be dark before you got back."

They were in the main room standing near the roll-top desk and now Karla glanced toward the open door. "I might have time."

Demery shook his head. "It'd be dark before you even *started* back."

"Well . . . I'll go in the morning then."

"Tomorrow's Sunday," her father reminded her. "They don't work on Sunday. So how're you going to get to him?"

"That's something you can't plan," Karla said. "A way just happens."

"Sis, even with your sunny outlook, how do you think it's going to just happen?"

"It happened the other day."

"You were lucky. Tomorrow they'll be standing in front of the barracks smoking, your friend one of them. Or maybe he'll be inside."

"If I don't see him tomorrow," Karla said, "then the next day. One more day isn't going to matter now that he's as good as out."

"You're taking a lot for granted. Lyall still has to prove his innocence."

"He will."

"You're sure of that."

"Pa, when something that looks almost impossible to start with all of a sudden turns possible and everything falls into place as if all you have to do is wish and it happens, then you know it's going to turn out all right."

"You figured that out all by yourself?"

"It makes sense."

"Do you know that your talking to him, even though he might be innocent—"

"Might be!"

"Listen to me. Your talking to him like that, even though

83

he might be innocent, is against the law. You know that, don't you?"

"Sending an innocent man to jail is against the law, too, if you all of a sudden want to be ethical about it."

"Karla, if I told you not to see him, but wait for Lyall to do something ... would you listen to me?"

"Of course I'd listen to you."

"But you'd go ahead and try to see him."

"It's only fair. If you were in prison, and were going to get out, wouldn't you want to know about it?"

"You're taking things for granted again," Demery reminded her.

"You just want to argue," Karla said.

Demery shook his head. "I'm glad I don't have your sweet faith in human nature."

"Some men," Karla said pointedly, "have to put on a big front of not believing in anything—hoping, I don't know why, that everybody will think they're very smart."

"You're some keen observer."

"If we had time, I'd tell you some other things."

"I guess you would," Demery said. "Listen, I'll tell you something now. I'll bet you four bits you don't talk to him tomorrow or the next day."

"You sound pretty sure of yourself."

"I'm just playing law of averages, Sis."

"Make it a dollar," Karla said, "and you've got a bet."

It was almost ten o'clock, the next morning, before Karla finished helping her father with the monthly report to the main office. She put aside the mail for the convict camp, then saddled her horse and brought it around to the front of the adobe. The next quarter of an hour was spent carrying in water from the pump to the big wooden tub in her bedroom. Her cold-water bath took only a few minutes and after it she brushed her hair and put on a fresh blouse and skirt.

John Demery's eyes studied her appraisingly as she came out of the bedroom. "Something special about today?"

Karla smiled. "I don't have time to be drawn into one of your traps."

"You're the only girl I know who can look dressed up in a man's shirt. Maybe if Willis had seen you, he would've stayed."

"Mr. Falvey was here?"

"He waved going by. Headed for the bar at Fuegos."

"The last time he was here," Karla said, "I think I frightened him. I told you—he was talking about wanting somebody to talk to—I felt sorry for him, but the way he was going about it I had to tell him to leave."

"Well, I don't imagine even his wife understands him," Demery said. He picked up the small bundle of convict camp mail from the desk and handed it to Karla. "There's a couple there for Willis. I didn't think about it . . . I could've given them to him."

"I'll give them to Lizann," Karla said.

"Don't get too close to her," Demery said. "Some of that gild might brush off."

"Now . . . you can't judge people just by looking at them."

"It seems to me I said the same thing not too long ago—about a man not having to look like a jailbird to be one."

Karla shook her head. "When you look at Corey Bowen, you know he's good. When you look at Lizann, you give her the benefit of the doubt." She leaned toward her father and kissed him on the cheek. "I'm going now. Before you think of something else to argue about."

She rode for the willow stand, passed through the dim silence of the trees, then entered the vast sunlight of the slope beyond and followed the sweeping curve of wagon tracks to the shoulder of the hill. There she left the tracks, riding straight on, up into the close-growing pines that covered the crest of the hill, following a horse trail now that twisted narrowly through the trees. Coming out of the trees, the horse trail dropped down a steeper grade, crossed the wagon ruts that had circled the hill, then followed the length of a narrow grama meadow before climbing again up through fields of house-sized boulders.

A mile farther on Karla emerged from a thin, steep-walled pass to stand above the canyon which the new road followed. Far below her, the dead end of the canyon was choked with pinyon and mesquite. The brush clumps thinned gradually as they spread and finally the dusty green patches of color disappeared completely, almost evenly, before reaching the end of new road construction.

Karla walked her horse along the west rim until she reached the trail that dropped down into the canyon: a rock-slide draw that fell to a shelf, the shelf hugging the wall narrowly until it reached the floor of the canyon. Karla descended and a quarter of a mile farther on, she stopped at the waterhole among the sycamores where she had talked to Bowen.

She let her horse drink. Coming out of the trees, her gaze caught the wisp of dust farther up canyon; but she reached the stretch of new road, passed the timbers that were used for grading, passed fire-blackened circles where brush had been burned, before she saw the rider who was leading the dust trail down the wash, down into the canyon and following the road now toward her.

It was Frank Renda. As she recognized him—her gaze going to him then sharply away from him—she saw the grave and the crude cross marking it off to the side of the canyon. Renda came directly toward her, making her rein in. His horse crowded Karla's and as their knees touched, Karla prodded her quirt at Renda's horse, backing away as she did.

Renda was smiling and he wiped the back of his hand over his heavy mustache. "This must be my day."

Karla was thinking of the new grave and she nodded to it, saying, "Someone was killed?" consciously making the question and the tone of her voice sound natural.

Renda followed her gaze. "Somebody tried to run away."

"Who was it?"

"What difference does it make?"

"I might have a letter for him," Karla said. She reached back, her hand touching the strap of the left-side saddlebag.

"His name was Miller," Renda said. Karla's hand hesitated on the strap. Now her fingers unfastened it and she drew out the bundle of letters. "You got something for him?"

She knew there was nothing for a Miller, but she loosened the string binding the letters and leafed through them. "None for that name."

"What about me?" Renda asked.

Karla glanced down and up again. "Nothing for you either."

"What's all the mail about then?"

"One for Mr. Brazil . . . one, two for Mr. Falvey."

"I'll take them back for you," Renda said.

Karla looked up. "It's all right. I'll take them. You go ahead wherever you're going."

Renda nodded to the letters. "That's where I was going. So I'm saving you a trip."

"I'd just as soon ride up and leave them myself," Karla said.

"There's no sense in that, if you don't have to."

She tried to smile. "I don't have anything to do anyway. Sunday's a funny day. There's nothing ever to do."

"Let me have the mail, Karla."

"Honestly, it's no trouble for me to ride to the camp. I *want* to."

"I don't care where you ride," Renda said. "Long as you give me the mail."

She was aware of his stare and the cold, threatening tone of his voice and only then did she realize that he wanted the letters for another reason, not simply to save her a trip to the camp. Still, she hesitated.

"Karla, you hand them over else I'll take them off you."

"If you're that anxious," Karla said, "all right." She leaned over to hand him the bundle then sat back in the saddle and watched him leaf through the envelopes. He pulled one of them out and looked at the return address on the envelope flap. Then, before Karla could speak, he had ripped open the envelope and was unfolding the letter.

"You can't read other people's mail!"

Not looking at her, Renda said, "Keep quiet."

"That's against the law!" Karla screamed. Then, more calmly, "Mr. Renda, you're tampering with the United States mail. You can go to prison for what you just did."

Renda looked up then. He was smiling and his eyebrows raised as if to show surprise. "I didn't know it was a personal letter."

"It wasn't addressed to you!"

Renda nodded calmly. "It was addressed to Willis. But Willis ain't at camp. What if it was something had to be tended to right away? Honey, it was my business to open it." He held up the second letter addressed to Falvey. "This one, too," he said, and tore it open.

The quirt, thonged to Karla's wrist, dropped from her hand as she kicked her horse against Renda's and reached for the letter. "Give me that!"

Renda pushed her and his horse side-stepped away. "Now don't get excited." She came at him again and he held her away until he finished reading the letter.

"No," Renda said. "That one wasn't business either." He grinned then. "It seems Willis put in for a transfer, but this"—he glanced down at the return address on the envelope—"Everett C. Allen, of Washington, D.C., thinks Willis ought to stay right here. Says there aren't any good openings now, but he'll let him know when one comes along and in the meantime, superintending a"—he looked down at the letter again—"a territorial penal institution was valuable experience and would equip him for a more responsible position when the opportunity presented itself."

Renda was still smiling. "Karla, did you know Five Shadows was a territorial penal institution?"

"My father's going to hear about this," Karla said.

"Your father's going to hear about it. Now that's something."

"You won't think it's funny then—opening other people's mail."

Renda crumpled both of the letters in his fist. "What mail?"

"Give me those!"

He held Karla away as she came at him again and threw the tight ball of paper over his shoulder. "I don't have anything, Karla. Just this pack of letters. That what you want?"

For a moment she stared at him, feeling a rage she could do nothing about. She dismounted then, looping her reins about the saddle horn, and walked around Renda's horse to pick up the crumpled letters.

"I'm giving this to my father," Karla said. "Just the way it is. You can count on a United States marshal visiting you within two weeks."

"Why? Because you found a piece of thrown-away paper?"

"You won't talk like that to a marshal."

"Whatever you're holding, I never saw before in my life," Renda said. "And you and all the United States marshals in the country aren't going to prove I did."

"We'll see," Karla said.

Renda swung down from the saddle and walked toward her. Watching him, Karla began to back away. "What's the matter with you?" Renda said. "I only want to give your letters back. You're so anxious to ride them up to the camp, all right. Here."

As Karla took them, Renda's hand went to her shoulder. "Karla, there's no good reason we have to fight."

"Take your hand off me."

"Why don't we just talk awhile. Get all the misunderstanding cleared away."

"I'm happy the way it is," Karla said. She shifted the mail to her left hand and her right hand closed around the quirt that hung from her wrist.

"Karla, we could go over and sit in that sycamore shade. Let the horses water—"

"I said take your hand off me!"

Renda grinned. "Like nobody ever touched you before."

The quirt came up. Before Renda saw it; the rawhide lashed across his face; before he could bring up his hands the whip came back stinging across his eyes, and as he covered his face Karla ran.

Five strides and she was in her saddle, spurring, reining tight to the left, cracking the quirt across the rump of Renda's mount, then at Renda as he ran to her, as he caught her leg, almost pulling her from the saddle. She swung viciously again and again, the quirt hissing, slashing at his straining upturned face, until suddenly he was no longer there.

As Renda went down, Karla's horse broke into a gallop. Over her shoulder she saw Renda on the ground, now rising to his feet and pausing to look after her, now running for his horse as it disappeared into the sycamore grove.

It rushed through Karla's mind that she was heading up canyon. To return home the way she had come, she would have to come about and run past Renda. He would have caught his horse by the time she passed the sycamores and would overtake her easily before she reached the end of the canyon. So there was no choice.

She would go to the camp. There were people there, and even if they worked for Renda it would be better there than being alone. He would follow her; but he would have had time to think of what he had done. Lizann would be there. She would tell Lizann about it and Frank Renda would have something else to think about. She could worry about returning home when the time came.

To her right, the wagon-trail wash came winding down through the talus and Karla reined toward it. Reaching the rim of the canyon she stopped long enough to look back. Far below her Renda, mounted again, was moving unhurriedly up the new stretch of road.

Minutes later, Karla was riding down the slope that stretched to the convict camp. The gate guard recognized her two hundred yards out. He unlocked the chain and swung half of the gate open to let Karla ride in.

"Is Mrs. Falvey home?"

The guard looked over toward the ramada. "That's her horse. I judge she's fixing for a ride."

"I want to deliver her mail," Karla said.

"Go right ahead, honey."

Karla dismounted. She glanced at the bundle of letters as if to leaf through them. "Maybe there's something for you."

The guard shook his head. "Don't take the bother to look."

"If you're that sure—" Karla said. She looked back as the guard started to swing the gate closed. He hesitated, squinting out into the glare and she knew he had seen the dust line coming down the slope.

"You might as well leave it open," Karla said.

Now they could make out the form of horse and rider. Still squinting the guard asked, "Who is it?"

"Your boss," Karla said. She moved away then, leading her horse toward the main adobe. Reaching the end of the building, she entered the shade of the ramada and moved along the edge of it to the support post where Lizann's horse stood. She half-hitched her reins to the post and walked over to the Falveys' quarters.

As she stepped into the doorway, Bowen and Lizann turned, moving apart, Lizann's arms coming down from Bowen's shoulders. Bowen's hand pushed into his shirt front, but not quickly enough. Karla had already seen the revolver in his hand.

TEN

"Renda's coming," Karla said tonelessly.

Bowen moved to the door. He looked out, then to Karla close to him in the doorway. "You didn't see anything, did you?"

She shook her head.

"Listen," Bowen said urgently. "I want to say a lot of things, but there isn't time. Just promise me you won't—"

"You'd better hurry," Karla said. Her eyes moved from Bowen's. She felt him brush past her. Then, when she turned, she saw him out beyond the two horses, walking across the yard toward the stable, glancing toward the gate as Renda entered the compound.

Lizann said, "Is he there?" She moved closer to the door in time to see Renda ride over to stop Bowen. There was a silence in the adobe as they watched the two men: Bowen standing in front of Renda's horse looking up at him and they could see that Renda was speaking. In front of the barracks, the convicts were watching and now the yard was quiet. They saw Renda step out of the saddle. Bowen's hand went to the front of his shirt and the hand scratched at his stomach idly. Renda was speaking. Bowen nodded. A minute passed, not more than a minute. Then, Bowen nodded again and turned away, going on toward the stable, as Renda caught up his reins and led his horse toward the adobe quarters.

Close to her, Karla heard a soft, exhaling sigh from Lizann. Karla's gaze remained on Bowen. She did not turn, not even when Lizann spoke.

"You and Corey have met before."

Karla nodded. "Did you give him the gun?"

"What gun?"

"That's not the way to help him!" Karla turned as she spoke.

"I don't know what you're talking about."

"I saw the gun—"

"You told Corey you didn't see anything."

"As far as anyone else is concerned."

91

"Why do you think *I* gave it to him?"

Karla glanced through the doorway, seeing Renda approaching, then back to Lizann. "Tell him not to use it. Please tell him that. Not now. Something has come up."

"You make very little sense," Lizann said.

"You don't have to understand it. Just tell him! If you wanted to help him enough to give him a gun then tell him!"

"Tell him what?"

"That the lawyer has found new evidence. Important enough to warrant a new trial. He's already filed the motion and it's only a matter of weeks—" Karla broke off hearing Renda's voice.

"Well...Miss Demery."

Lizann turned back into the room. She went to the canvas chair and sat down. Karla stepped back from the doorway as Renda entered.

"Why don't you come in?" Lizann said. "Make yourself at home."

Renda looked at her. "What're you edgy about...something this girl told you?"

"She hasn't told me anything."

He turned to Karla. "You change your mind about causing a fuss?"

"I told you what I'm going to do."

"You want me to tell Lizann?" Renda asked.

"If you don't," Karla said. "I will."

"You could be a damn sight easier to get along with." He looked at Lizann again. "I opened a couple of Willis's letters by mistake, but Karla thinks I done it on purpose."

"You know he did," Karla said.

"So Karla thinks she's going to make trouble for me," Renda went on. "Going to tell her father about it. And claims he'll call in a federal marshal. So if Karla's going to go to all that trouble, I'm not about to admit reading the letters. Am I, Lizzy?"

"You're admitting it right now," Karla said. "In front of Mrs. Falvey."

Renda's gaze moved to Lizann. "Did you hear me admit anything?" Lizann said nothing and Renda's eyes returned to Karla. "If a federal marshal stopped by here, Lizzy wouldn't know anything about it."

Karla began, "When I tell Mr. Falvey—"

"And Willis," Renda broke in, "will tell the marshal that he read the letters and threw them away when he was finished, and if some girl out for a ride happened to find them, that's no concern of his. All Willis will know is that he threw the letters away. You see how it is, honey?"

Karla looked at Lizann who returned her gaze almost without expression, telling nothing, least of all offering assistance. Then, to Renda again, "I don't see how you have the nerve to admit what you just did."

Renda shrugged. "You're the only one hearing it. You got no witnesses. I got a man who'll admit reading the letters and throwing them away for you to find."

"You're very sure of yourself," Karla said.

"Honey, when you're minding thirty convicts you got to be sure of yourself."

"I'm still going to tell my father."

"You go right ahead...And tell him for me, I want to know the day my supplies come in this week. I don't want them laying around for some stage passenger to drop a cigar butt on. You hear me? Soon as they come in, I want to know about it."

"You'll notice," Lizann said mildly, "he's worried about his investment and not your station."

"I'll hear from you in a minute," Renda said. He looked at Karla again. "You run home now. And remember what I said. Soon as it comes in I want to know about it."

"I'm dismissed now?" Karla said.

"You're double dismissed. Ride directly through that gate and don't let me see your face around here till my stuff comes."

"Mr. Renda," Karla said, "you're a real gentleman."

Renda smiled pleasantly. "Thank you, Karla. Now get out before I kick you the hell out!" He saw her about to speak and he yelled, "Go on!" then kept his eyes on her until she had left the adobe, mounted her horse and ridden off toward the gate.

Lizann asked, "What did all that prove?"

"When somebody talks like that," Renda said, "I get sick to my stomach."

"Maybe it's your conscience backing up on you."

"A sermon now?"

Lizann shook her head. "Not even if I thought it would do you good."

Renda moved to the table. He half sat on the edge of it, hooking his leg over one corner, and leaned his weight heavily against the table. Watching him, still sitting in the canvas chair, Lizann said, "Don't make yourself too comfortable."

"I thought we'd have a talk," Renda said.

"About what?"

"Willis's letters."

"I'm not interested."

"You want me to think you're not," Renda said. "You're bustin' to know what was in them."

"Then keep it to yourself," Lizann said, "and see if I bust."

"They were from Washington."

"I told you, I'm not interested."

Renda came to his feet. "I'm interested! You understand that? I'm interested and we're going to damn-well talk about them whether you want to or not!"

"As usual," Lizann said calmly, "you'll be talking to yourself."

The table creaked as Renda leaned his weight on it again. "Let's find out," he said mildly, and noticed the look of momentary surprise on Lizann's face. "We don't have to yell at each other, Lizzy. Pretend you're in Washington and you're talking to one of Willis's political friends. Like Mr. Everett C. Allen."

"The letters were from him?"

"That's better," Renda grinned.

"Were they?"

"They were from him."

"What did he say?"

"He was answering Willis."

"I didn't know Willis had written him."

"You expect me to believe that?"

"I don't care what you believe!"

"You should. It makes a difference."

"I didn't know Willis had written to him," Lizann said evenly. "You can believe that or not."

"Let's say I don't. Who is he?"

"Everett? He's with the Department of the Interior."

"High up?"

"High enough."

"High enough to get Willis away from here?"

Lizann nodded. "What did he say?"

Renda's leg, hooked over the corner of the table, began to swing slowly back and forth. He stared at Lizann and for perhaps a full minute he said nothing. Then, "What're you so anxious to know for? You don't even know what Willis said to him first."

"Does it matter?" Lizann asked.

"You know damn well it matters."

"If you are going to insist that I know what Willis wrote," said Lizann, "there's no use discussing it further."

"I'll bet you even told him what to write."

Lizann sat lower in her chair. Her gaze went to the open doorway and she ignored Renda.

"I'll bet Willis didn't even want to write it. But you made him."

Lizann's gaze came back to Renda. "Willis asked for a transfer!"

"That's pretty good," Renda said. "You must've been rehearsing—opening your big brown eyes, looking surprised—"

"What did Everett say," Lizann demanded.

"What do you think he said?"

Lizann hesitated thoughtfully. "Something to the effect that Willis was gaining valuable experience . . . that there were no openings elsewhere, but when the right opportunity presented itself—"

"You know this man pretty well," Renda said.

"I have seen his letters before."

"So Willis is stuck," Renda said. "I told him that a long time ago."

Lizann said nothing.

"I told him. I said, 'Willis, relax and enjoy it. You're gaining valuable experience here and if you do good, maybe they'll make you superintendent at my next camp.'"

"God help him," Lizann murmured.

"That could happen, Lizzy."

"I wish you wouldn't call me that."

"It bothers you?"

"How do you know there's going to be a next camp?"

"Same way I got this one."

"You bribed someone for the contract?"

"That's a bad word."

"You must have."

95

"Mine was low bid, Lizzy."

"You know nothing about road construction. Someone must have told you what to bid—for a price. Someone on the inside."

Renda grinned. "A silent partner."

"What I don't understand," Lizann said, "is why you bother. You have to use bribes. You have to watch every move anyone makes. You hire a man like Brazil, who would come higher than the ordinary guard. You're constantly in danger of being found out. For what?"

"For fifteen dollars a day profit, free and clear," Renda said.

"Which isn't very much," Lizann said.

"Besides what I make on the road contract."

"But with your expenses, there couldn't be much left of that."

"Enough," Renda said. "Which adds on to the fifteen a day—"

"How do you come to that amount?"

"The government subsistence!" He sounded surprised that she had to ask. "I don't know why they think each man's worth seventy cents a day—when you only need about twenty cents to take care of one. But as long as they want to pay it, I'll make my fifteen a day. Figure that back over four months. Then go ahead a couple more months. See how it adds up? I figure I'll make three thousand on that alone...something I didn't even count on when I got the contract."

"Do you think it's worth the effort?"

"Lizzy, I'm not straining. I sit in the shade all day counting my money. When this job's over, I spend the money. Then I get another contract."

"Considering the chances you're taking," Lizann said, "I would think you'd play for higher stakes."

"Why? I'm not greedy."

"How much do you pay my husband?"

"Whatever I feel like, now."

"Just enough to keep him drunk."

"He started low." Renda grinned. He said then, "You better have a talk with Willis about his letter writing. I don't want to hear any more about trying to get transferred."

"If it bothers you," Lizann said, "talk to him yourself."

"Lizzy, I'm being nice about this. I don't have to be."

"What Willis does is no concern of mine," Lizann said evenly. "I want to make that clear to you. As far as I'm concerned, Willis doesn't exist. At one time I wanted him to leave here and I tried to persuade him with every argument I could think of. Willis was afraid to do anything—afraid for his life and afraid for what he chooses to call his career. So I stopped trying to persuade him. Willis is on his own—and I'm on my own."

"Well," Renda said pleasantly, "if it's all right with you, I'll still consider you and Willis a pair. Whatever he does, you're behind it; and whatever you do, he at least knows about it. As long as you're living together that makes it easier to keep track of both of you."

Lizann nodded. "As long as we're living together."

Renda studied her. "Is that supposed to mean something?"

"Think it over."

"I don't have to. I'm asking you."

"You'll find out soon enough."

"Lizann . . . now don't do anything you'll be sorry for."

"It's already done. And I won't be sorry."

"What're you talking about?"

"Wait and see."

"I don't wait on anybody!" Renda came off the table. "I'm telling you right now, if you're planning to leave, forget about it. You try anything, I'll fix you once and for all!"

"Frank," Lizann said patiently. "I've already told you how I feel about Willis. You can ruin him, cause him to go to prison, and it won't make the least difference to me."

"Who says I'm talking about Willis?"

"You've been holding him over me like a club."

Renda shook his head. "Let's get it right out in plain sight. Lizzy, I'll tell you one time and one time only." His hand came up and he pointed a finger at her. "You try to leave here without my knowing about it, I'll kill you." His hand dropped. "It's that cut and dried."

Slowly, Lizann shook her head and her expression was composed as she said, "I'm going to leave here, Frank. And there won't be a thing you'll be able to do about it."

"You're bluffing," Renda said.

"Am I? You'll see." Lizann smiled then. "Start thinking about it now—go over in your mind every possible way I could leave here—and you'll still be thinking about it when it happens."

ELEVEN

THE NEW ROAD had reached as far as the sycamore grove the morning Manring arranged to work with Bowen's stump-pulling detail.

He waited until the wagons were unloaded and the convicts had moved off before he went over to Frank Renda, who had dismounted and was standing near the equipment wagon.

Manring touched the brim of his straw work hat. "Mr. Renda—"

"What do you want?"

Manring leaned over the end gate of the equipment wagon then, reaching for the handle of a shovel. "I want to work with the stump pullers."

Renda rolled a fresh cigar between his lips and clamped it in the corner of his mouth. He moved leisurely to the end of the wagon to scratch a match against the gate board. "Before," Renda said, "it was to get off that job."

"I'm not talking about permanent," Manring murmured. "Put me on it a couple of days . . . long enough to find something out."

"What've you heard?"

"Nothing yet. Bowen and Ike got their heads together. That's all I know. Set me with them a couple of days and we'll know more."

"What's your price this time?"

"I'll let you know. After I think about it."

"Keep talking like that," Renda said, "your price'll be the punishment cell."

Manring's eyes raised briefly. "Look, I don't have time to be polite. Either put me with them or don't."

"They find out what you're doing," Renda said, "some morning we'll shovel you out of the barracks."

"That's my worry."

"I know it is," Renda said. "I'm just curious to know what you want in return. You got about the softest job now—riding that scraper."

"If I'm going to pull stumps," Manring said impatiently, "I better get at it."

"Go ahead."

"I'll have to get rid of the Mexican."

Renda nodded. "Send him over. I'll put him on the scraper." He watched Manring shoulder the long-handled shovel and walk off toward Bowen's group.

Now another one to watch, Renda thought. And he wondered if it was worth it. You didn't trust anybody in this business, least of all a man who would inform on his own kind. Still, a man like that could be valuable and sometimes having one around was worth it, even if you couldn't trust him.

Manring had been right about Bowen planning to jump the supply wagon that day. It had marked the beginning of Manring as an informer. And it was a strange beginning, because he had given the information without first asking for a reward. It was not until days later, after Bowen and Ike were in the punishment cell, that he asked to be taken off the stump-pulling detail. And then only hinted that perhaps he would learn other things that would be worth passing along.

Because he had been right the first time, there was no reason to doubt Manring now. That Bowen and Pryde might be up to something made considerable sense. Some men you could beat till your arms fell off and they still wouldn't learn. Bowen had tried it once. You could tell by looking at him that he had the itch to run, and you could bet safely that he'd try it again.

And Pryde. Serving thirty years. Only six of them behind him. Thirty years for killing a man with a broken whisky bottle in a saloon fight. Yes, Pryde qualified. With twenty-four years to go—no time off—he'd be more likely to run than Bowen. But Ike would be more choosy about how the break would be made, because he had more time to think about it.

So let Manring snoop, Renda thought. Make him tell whatever he learns. And if his price is out of line, then throw him the hell in solitary. Let him think it over by himself. He thought then: Which is what you ought to do with Lizann.

But you wouldn't be sure of Willis's reaction. Willis was

weak, and by now too whisky-soaked to think for himself. But if something were to happen to Lizann— No, you couldn't be sure what Willis would do . . . even afraid as he was.

Since his talk with Lizann, Renda had thought it out very carefully. There were only two ways she could leave Five Shadows. Either try to run away by herself, or try to summon help from the outside. Both of these avenues were blocked. He read every piece of mail she wrote or received and a Mimbre followed her whenever she took her sorrel out. So Renda told himself she was bluffing. She was being wearisome, trying to get him excited, because there was nothing she could do about her situation.

Still, as Lizann had predicted, he continued to think about it, and merely telling himself that she was bluffing did not ease his mind.

Manring was confident now that Renda would believe almost anything he might tell him. That was a sign that his luck as still running. No, it wasn't all luck. Getting in with Renda wasn't luck. Arousing Bowen's interest in the dynamite wasn't luck either. It was work and thinking and sweating and being five jumps ahead of any luck that could turn against you.

The luck had been in the beginning. First, seeing the basis of a plan come apart with the word that Bowen was ready to run. Bowen the dynamiter, without whom the plan was nothing. So there had been no choice and informing on Bowen had been a good way to test his luck.

Manring reasoned it this way: If Bowen escaped, or, if he were killed in the attempt, the dynamite plan was finished. But if Renda knew beforehand that Bowen was going, they would be ready for him and Bowen would have only a slim chance at best. He *might* be killed; but, to Manring, the odds leaned slightly toward his being taken alive. Perhaps with gunshot wounds, but nevertheless alive.

As it happened, Bowen was taken and Manring's luck began its run. That he had tested his luck with a man's life in the balance rose to his conscience only briefly. He shrugged it off with the thought that if Bowen had been killed, he deserved it. He would be repaid for that night in the Prescott jail cell: the night Bowen slugged him four times before the deputy pulled him off.

It was not until a few days after Bowen and Pryde had been thrown into the punishment cell that Manring realized that he had not asked Renda for a reward. He could not risk Renda suspecting that he had informed on Bowen for any other reason than for a reward. So he asked to be taken off stump pulling.

Now he was doing the same thing in reverse. Nearing the end of the canyon, it was time to be working with Bowen again. When the dynamite arrived he would still be with Bowen. Renda would be asking what he had learned and he would have to stall Renda. But that could be done, he was sure. And Pryde. It was too bad Ike was still working with Bowen. But maybe something would happen to Ike.

Bowen was backing the team into position, Pryde pushing down on the long handle of his shovel, levering the stump, and the Mexican was passing the chain through the stump's shallow roots. Pryde saw him first. He said, "Here comes Earl." And now the three of them paused. They waited expectantly, watching Manring coming toward them.

As he reached them, Manring's eyes went to the Mexican and he lowered the shovel. "Renda wants to see you."

The Mexican's hand moved to his chest. "Me? What does he want with me?"

"Don't get overheated. You're going on the scraper."

"On the scraper? But why does he want *me?*"

"Ask him. I don't run the place."

The Mexican rose slowly, wiping his hands on his thighs. "Maybe he thinks I did something that I didn't do."

"You're going on the *scraper.* That isn't punishment."

The Mexican shook his head. "Something's wrong."

"You're just jumpy," Manring said.

"I'm jumpy since the time Chick Miller went to see Renda."

"Go on, get out of here."

Manring's eyes followed the Mexican as he started off toward the equipment wagon, then his gaze returned. He looked from Pryde to Bowen as he said, "I got transferred."

Bowen only nodded, but Pryde said, "We saw you talking to Renda."

"Sure. He was sending me over here."

101

"You're talking to him all the time, aren't you?"

Manring looked over at Bowen. "Your friend don't trust me."

"Maybe I don't either," Bowen said. He backed the team up to the stump and there was no more said until they had pulled the stump and Pryde moved off with the team, dragging the stump to the nearest bonfire.

Manring said then, "I talked Renda into sending me over here. We got to be working together, Corey, if we're going to pull it."

"You can talk in front of Ike," Bowen said. "I already told him about it."

"You told Ike!"

"He wants to get out just like you do."

"We don't need three!"

"But you need me. And if Ike doesn't go, I don't."

"Corey . . . it's different with you and me. We got no business being here in the first place. Ike *killed* a man. He *deserves* to be here."

"I'm not judging him," Bowen said. "If I go, so does Ike."

By late afternoon, the road had passed the sycamore grove and was halfway to the horse trail that slanted gradually up the western tree-covered slope of the canyon.

"By tomorrow afternoon the brush cutters will be on the slope," Manring said. His shovel jabbed at the roots of the stump they were working on. As Bowen went to his knees, Manring stooped, pushing down on the shovel and one side of the stump lifted, popping the roots that held it. Pryde passed the end of the chain to Bowen and they fastened it to the stump. As they worked, their eyes would raise to the tree-covered slant of the canyon wall looming above them.

"More or less," Manring said, "the road's got to follow that natural trail."

Pryde said, "I don't see any trail. Though it must be there. The girl passes this way and so does Willis."

"You can't see it for the trees," Manring said. "It goes up a shelf, all the way up, that looks like it was put there for the purpose. When the trees are cleared, maybe the shelf would be wide enough for a wagon. But it'd be *just* wide enough, without any room to spare."

"So," Bowen said. "You blast the wall out and use the rock to build up the shoulder of the road."

"That's the way I see it," Manring said.

"Is that the way you and Renda both see it?" Bowen said.

"What do you mean by that?"

"You and he surveyed it together, didn't you? Is that the way Renda said it would be done?"

"Something like that," Manring said guardedly. "He wasn't sure and he just talked about it generally."

"So you weren't sure either how it would be done," Bowen said.

"As sure as anybody," Manring insisted. "There's only one way to get out."

"We want to hear your idea," Bowen said.

"You're awful damn anxious. We got about a week yet."

"Earl, I don't think you have a plan."

"You'll find out."

Bowen nodded. "We'll find out right now."

"It'd be easier to tell it once we got up on the slope."

"Earl, I think you're stalling."

"I can't give you details now! You got to be up there to see what I'm talking about, else it won't mean anything to you."

"Try us anyway," Bowen said.

"Well," Manring began, "it's based on three things. We got to do three things else it isn't going to work." He spoke slowly, as if giving himself time to think.

"First we got to take care of the guard that'll be on us. I figure Renda or Brazil. We get hold of him, but without anybody else knowing about it. Second, we set the charge so as to close the road on anybody coming up from below. Lay a rock slide over it or else blow a hole in it that a horse couldn't cross. Third, we got to take care of the Mimbres. I figure we can force Renda or Brazil, whichever one we're holding, to call them out. See, we'll have another charge planted. All this is timed to the second and just as they come out—boom—they're blown sky-high."

"Then what?" Bowen said.

"Then we run for the station. For horses."

Bowen looked at Pryde. "What do you think?"

"He don't anymore have a plan than I do."

"He must've just thought it up," Bowen said.

Manring looked from one to the other. "What're you trying to pull?"

"You got a lot of holes in your idea," Bowen said. "That's all."

"Well, sure," Manring said. "You can't work everything out until you got the stuff."

"You can't work anything out," Bowen said.

"It'll go like I said, or it won't go at all."

"Maybe some of it will," Bowen said. "You've wanted us to believe you had a plan so we'd get it in our heads we need you. You supplying the brains and Ike and me lighting the fuse. But it comes out all you have is a sketchy idea . . . and now we're not sure if we do need you, Earl."

Manring remained calm, as if he had anticipated this and already knew how he would answer it. He shook his head saying, "You won't do it without me. If you don't like my idea, think it's got holes, then figure your own way. But whatever way you do it, I'm going to be along."

"Now he's threatening us," Pryde said.

"You can call it whatever you want," Manring said.

Pryde shrugged. "I was thinking you wouldn't want to go up there with us. A man could fall and kill himself."

"Ike," Manring said, "I can fix it for you right now."

"You're going, Earl," Bowen said easily. "We might not need your help, but we sure as hell need you in plain sight."

As Manring predicted, the "brush cutters"—the convicts who cleared the pinyon and scrub brush—were working their way up the slope by midafternoon of the next day. On the morning of the day after that, the crews that followed, including the scraper, had reached the beginning of the trail and could go no farther—not until dynamite widened the narrow, uneven horse trail. But the dynamite had not yet arrived.

By noon, two thirds of the convicts were idle—until Renda devised something for them to do. He was reluctant to put more men up on the slope. That would increase the rate of construction, shorten the job time and consequently decrease his daily profit. Still, the convicts had to be kept busy. So he put them to work clearing the canyon area beyond the point at which the road would begin ascending the west slope.

"Cleaning out the brush is for your own good," Renda told the convicts. "Then later on when we're working high up and somebody falls off, we'll be able to find the body for a decent burial."

There were three bonfires to consume the brush as it was hacked down and cleared away. Bowen was given the job of tending one of them. Shirtless in the close, almost unbearable heat, he would throw the dry brush into the flames. Then, waiting for more to be dragged over to him, his gaze would raise to the jagged, climbing trace of the horse trail that became visible, foot by foot, as the pinyon was toppled into the canyon.

Now it was a matter of patience, of waiting and using the time to think it out clearly, to think of every possibility. No, there was not that much time—not time to think of everything—so you eliminated some of the things right away. The things you had thought of already and had seen no hope in. Like Karla... and the lawyer... and walking out with a pardon or a parole or an acquittal or whatever you wanted to call it.

It was nice to think about that. It was nice to think about her. But it didn't do you any good. And now you think about only the things that'll do you some good. And it's the bad things that do you good. Do you realize that? You get good from bad. That isn't possible, but that's what you're getting. From Lizann. And from Earl.

A gun from Lizann and an idea from Earl.

Bowen had hidden the gun in the stable. In the stall where Renda's chestnut mare was kept, he had pried loose one of the boards against the back wall and slipped the gun behind it. There, because the barracks offered no safe place to hide it. Getting it again, when the time came, would be another problem.

But there were a lot of problems and one more didn't make much difference. Shooting Willis Falvey, though, was not one of the problems.

Lizann's plan, when he realized it, was very simple. It was not a question of running away. That had no part in it. If her husband were killed, there would be an investigation. Someone would come down from Prescott—if not for a formal investigation, at least to take over Willis's duties. When he did, Lizann would leave, and Renda would be able to do nothing about it. It was that simple. A convict, trying to escape, had killed Willis. The convict either got away or was recaptured. That was the convict's problem.

But it won't be your problem, Bowen thought. And it

won't be anybody else's problem, unless she had more than one gun.

He imagined that she would be confident, patiently waiting for it to happen, rehearsing what she would say to the man from Prescott—perhaps even taunting Renda with hints that she would be leaving soon.

Lizann had a surprise coming.

So you are left with Earl. Earl and the dynamite. And you have to be careful how you mix them if you expect to get out of this alive.

On the morning of the second day of tending the brush fire, Bowen saw Karla Demery ride down into the canyon. The convicts on the slope stopped working to watch her go by; and those below, on the floor of the canyon, turned and followed her with their eyes as she crossed to Renda sitting in a shaded section of the east wall.

She spoke to Renda for only a moment, then reined her horse in a tight circle. As she did, her gaze found Bowen. She nudged her horse toward the fire, toward the motionless naked-to-the-waist figure who stood in front of the swirling, wind-caught rise of smoke. Renda called to her and she drew in the reins. Bowen watched. She was not more than fifty feet away, still looking toward him. She wanted to tell him something, he could see that by her expression. Then it was too late. Renda, mounted now, came up next to her and they rode off together toward the nearest team of horses.

A few minutes later they passed Bowen again, heading up the canyon. Behind them came a wagon carrying three convicts, one of them Manring. A guard followed, bringing up the rear.

She wanted to tell you something, Bowen thought. But it could've been bad news as easily as good, so don't think about it. You've got enough to figure out already. But through the rest of the day his thoughts would go to Karla Demery. She was not that easily put from his mind.

That evening the convicts were in the barracks when the wagon returned. Six men were called out to help unload it and they did not return for over a half hour. When they did, Manring was with them.

The lean, bearded man came over to Bowen's mat. He sat down at the foot of it and rolled a cigarette. "Let me have a match."

Bowen handed him a box of matches and watched silently.

Manring struck the match. As he held it to his cigarette he said, "Boy, we just unloaded it in the stable. Enough to blow everybody clean to hell."

TWELVE

"WAIT A MINUTE," Renda called. "This is far enough!" He brought up his shotgun as the four men on the climbing trail ahead of him stopped.

Brazil, leading the file, called back, "He says you got to start at the top."

"You believe everything he tells you?" Renda's face, flushed from the climb, showed sudden anger.

To Bowen who was second in line, carrying two coils of fuse over his shoulder and a box of detonators in his hand, Brazil said, "The old man can't take it, so he's got to yell at somebody."

Bowen turned and looked past Pryde and Manring who followed him to Renda. "You want to stand here with fifty pounds of dynamite and talk about it?"

Renda edged along the inside of the trail close to the wall, past Manring and Pryde. As he reached Bowen, Pryde lowered the case of dynamite from his shoulder, placed it against the wall and sat down on it.

Manring, carrying a shovel, a hand axe and a sapling pole, looked at him uncertainly. "You better be careful."

As Manring spoke, Renda turned quickly. "What are you doing!"

"I'm resting," Pryde said, "while you talk it out."

"You can't sit on dynamite!"

"And I can't stand with it a hunnert feet above nowhere while you get over your nervous state."

Bowen said to Renda, "I explained it once. You got to start at the top."

"He don't take to high places," Pryde said. "Or marching behind fifty pounds of charge."

Renda turned on him angrily. "Pick it up!"

Pryde remained seated, leaning back against the wall. "There's more chance of dropping it than my hind-end heat setting it off."

"I said pick it up!" The tight-muscled, open-eyed expression of Renda's face was dark with anger. He was aware of the four men watching him, and wanting to show neither anger nor fear he said to Bowen, more calmly, "All right. We'll talk about it upstairs."

Rising, lifting the case of explosives, Pryde said, "Frank, you want to carry this a while?"

But Renda, refusing to be angered further, ignored Pryde. He remained in line where he stood and followed Bowen the rest of the way up the trail, along the slanting wall, then into a depression where the rock had fallen away and the trail was less steep. The depression cut into the wall and formed a forty-foot draw from the shelf up to the rim of the canyon.

As he came up out of the draw, Bowen saw a Mimbreño tracker off in the trees. He was there for a moment, then gone. That's your big problem, Bowen thought.

Renda was breathing heavily as he reached level ground. He stepped aside as Pryde and Manring came up and said to Bowen, "All right, why do you start at the top?"

"I figure—" Bowen began.

"You figure!"

"I never blew up a mountain before."

Renda exhaled. "Go on."

"I figure," Bowen said again, emphasizing the word, "If you start from the bottom, as you work up you'll be covering what you just uncoverd every time you set a blast. You get your road widened and the shoulder built up, then touch one off higher up and"—he snapped his finger—"like that, no more road."

Manring said, "That makes sense."

Renda glanced at him. Then to Bowen he said, "What do you do first?"

"Test the fuse." Bowen placed the box of detonators on the ground carefully and took the two coils of fuse from his arm, dropping one of them and handing the end of the other fuse to Manring. Then he walked away from them, straightening the line as he did, measuring it with the length of his hand as he unwound it. With ten feet of it played out he said to Renda, "I need a knife."

"What for?"

"To cut the fuse!"

"I'll do the cutting."

Bowen shrugged. "Then over the next couple of weeks you're going to be living on an awful lot of dynamite."

Renda brought out a pocket knife. He hesitated, then

handed it to Bowen. "Every day when we quit, you give this back to me. Closed."

Bowen smiled. "You don't trust anybody." He cut the fuse, then stretched it out on the ground. "Have you got a clock with a sweep hand on it?" When Renda nodded, Bowen said, "Start timing as soon as it catches." He pulled a match from his hatband, struck it on the bottom of his shoe and touched it to the fuse.

The fuse hissed and a small flame spurted from the end of it. There was little smoke, but the fuse moved and seemed alive with the flame burning through its powder-filled core. "It's slow enough," Renda said.

"Mind your clock," Bowen told him. When the fuse had burned all the way, he looked at Renda again. "How long?"

"About three minutes."

"Mr. Renda," Bowen said mildly, "we're talking about how much time to get clear of a blast. Don't give me any *about.*"

Renda glared at him, but looked at his watch again and said, "Just a little over three minutes. Maybe five seconds."

After a moment Bowen said, "That means it burns just about a foot in eighteen seconds. Maybe you think that's slow. It's not when you're lighting the end of it."

"I'm impressed," Renda said. "Now what?"

"Now we'll test the charges," Bowen answered. Manring drew the hand axe from his belt and handed it to Bowen as he moved to the case of dynamite. On the top of the case was stenciled, *This Side Up,* below that, *High Explosives— Dangerous,* and at the end which Bowen opened, *50 lbs. No. 1 Dynamite—1¼ x 8 inches.*

"You're supposed to use a wooden hammer and wedge to open this," Bowen said.

Renda edged toward him, then back again. "Why?"

"Something about a metal tool slipping and hitting the charge," Bowen said, prying the top boards loose with the hand axe. "You never know what'll happen."

Renda's hands were tight about the shotgun and he stood without moving. "We don't need any talk. Just hurry it up."

"That's another rule," Bowen said. "You don't hurry." He lifted one of the ten paraffin-coated packets from the case and opened it. "Here you are," Bowen said. He extended one of the dynamite cartridges to Renda.

"I don't want it!"

"I thought maybe you wanted to see one close." Bowen rose and glanced around, then moved to the edge of the draw and looked down, studying the narrow defile that reached to the trail.

"Earl," Bowen said then. "Take your stick down there and poke a hole in the left-hand wall. Right down at the end of it."

"How deep?"

"Deep as you can make it. Start about a yard in from the corner." As Manring started down the defile, Brazil following him, Bowen cut a three-foot length of fuse. He opened the box of detonators, took one of the copper capsules from its felt wrapping and begn to gently push the fuse into the capsule's open end. He did this very carefully until the fuse was touching the detonating compound. Then, with his teeth, he crimped the open end of the detonator tightly to the fuse.

Pryde said, "You ought'n to use your mouth for that."

"I don't see any nippers around," Bowen said, and thought: For a man in the construction business he's missing a damn awful lot of tools.

"How many sticks?" asked Pryde.

"We'll try three," Bowen said. "And find a stick—sharp pointed and about the size of a pencil." He moved down the draw then, holding the detonator gently in his closed hand. Pryde followed, but Renda came only halfway down.

Brazil stepped back as Bowen reached them. He saw Renda then and called, "What's the matter, Frank?"

"Mind what you're paid for!"

Brazil was grinning. "You're going to miss something way up there."

"I can see all right." Renda was twenty feet up the draw standing close to one of the steeply sloping banks.

"That deep enough?" Manring asked. "The stick's no damn good."

"You'll have to get a metal rod," Bowen said. He looked closely at the hole. It was formed in a slanting crevice in the rock and was not really a hole at all, only the rock fragments cleared from the crevice, but it would serve the purpose.

Pryde handed him two cartridges and Bowen inserted them into the seam. As he did he murmured, "Look around,

Ike. Get the lay of things. Figure how the Mimbres would come from the other side of the canyon."

He unwrapped one end of the third cartridge and with the pinyon twig that Pryde gave him punched a small hole. The detonator went into this, and Bowen rewrapped the paraffin-coated paper so that only the tip of the detonator, with the fuse extending from it, could be seen. This went into the crevice, then loose sand on top of it so there would be no space between the charges and the walls of the crevice. Bowen tamped the sand gently and now they were ready.

He looked down into the canyon—seeing the convicts grouped around the wagons that were pulled over to the far side and the two guards mounted and standing off from them—then lit the fuse. As he turned he saw Renda go over the top of the draw. "Frank's already cleared," Brazil said, then waited to go up last to show that he wasn't afraid.

They moved back from the rim of the canyon and a moment later the blast went off. Dust billowed up out of the draw and close on the explosion they heard the faint boom of an echo up canyon, then another, then silence and the dust hung in the sunlight above them.

As it began to clear, they went down into the draw again. The corner that met the trail was sheered off in an undercut. Shattered rock and sand were scattered over the shelf and much of it had gone over the edge into the canyon.

"That wasn't so big," Renda said. He was at ease again.

"The next one'll be bigger," Bowen said. "First you find out what a few sticks will do. Then you add to it." He glanced at Pryde, then back to Renda. "We can make them as big as you want."

Bowen organized the routine and that day they blasted three times. At Bowen's direction they began thirty feet down the trail from the defile. Four convicts were brought up and put to work digging into the wall of the canyon. Their job was to hollow a niche six feet deep and wide enough for Manring to work in. Manring would then cut a hole, parallel with the canyon wall, for the dynamite charges. As he did this, the four convicts would return to the bottom of the canyon.

Renda said, why not send them around into the draw? But Bowen objected. "Once we light the fuse that's the way we run, and we're not going to have anybody standing around in the way." There was an anxious moment, a moment of seeing the plan that was already forming go to nothing. "That's why we started down a ways," Bowen explained, "instead of right at the defile. So we'd have cover to use. But it won't do us any good crowded with men." Renda said nothing and Bowen added, "Then, after we're about halfway down the trail and working the dynamite from the bottom, we'll come back and blow the part we skipped. Right now, though, we got to have that pass clear."

Renda thought it over. "All right," he said finally, "send them down before you set your charge"—and Bowen's anxiety was past.

They exploded the first charge at midmorning—a forty-pound charge with the cartridges tied into bundles of eight—and the convicts were kept busy until almost noon clearing the shattered rock, spreading it evenly over the widened section of road.

As Bowen thought would happen, Renda went below before the first charge was set off, leaving Brazil to watch them. Brazil remained close. He would wait until the fuse was lighted, then go for the draw with them. He seemed fascinated by the dynamite, by the force and the noise of it, and he watched every phase of the work carefully.

That afternoon they moved a dozen feet farther down the trail. This would be slow going, Bowen realized, blowing only ten or twelve feet at a time; but Renda did not have drilling equipment and without it they could use only smaller charges effectively. Another niche was carved out of the crusted sand and rock and another blast set off. Then later, after the third charge was exploded, after watching Brazil and now realizing there would be only one more day of using the draw for cover, Bowen made up his mind.

And later again, in the barracks that evening, after the lamps had been put out and the three of them crouched in the darkness beneath the window, Bowen explained his escape plan. He told Pryde and Manring exactly what each of them would do. He made sure there were no objections. He emphasized that each man had to do what he was supposed to do, and nothing else. And if they did, this would be their last night at Five Shadows.

THIRTEEN

SIX HUNDRED POUNDS of dynamite were brought out of the stable and loaded onto the equipment wagon the next morning. Bowen specified the amount. He remained in the stable until the wagon was loaded and when he came out he was carrying four detonator boxes. One of the boxes had been emptied and in it was Lizann Falvey's .25-caliber Colt.

Bowen drove the equipment wagon. He took it over the Five Shadows slope, down into the canyon and to the foot of the trail that reached silently up into the early morning sunlight. The floor of the canyon was in shadow and there was little talk as the dynamite was unloaded.

"We'll take eight cases up," Bowen told Renda. "Leave the other four down here. Maybe we'll use them, but I don't think so."

Renda pointed to eight men in turn, and approximately fifteen minutes later the dynamite was up on the rim of the canyon. The eight men returned to the convicts working on the ledge, spreading the results of the previous day's last explosion. And now the dynamite crew was alone with Brazil.

They were ready to plant the first charge when Willis Falvey came up the trail. He passed them without a word, without even looking to see what they were doing, kicked his dun horse up through the draw and rode along the rim until he was beyond the end of the canyon.

The way you're going, Bowen thought, watching him disappear into the deep shadow of the pass which led down to the boulder field beyond the canyon.

Through a mile of rocks and across the meadow, Bowen thought. Up past the road, straight over the hill and down the grade. Cross the creek, come out of the willows. You're there.

Brazil's voice brought him back to the ledge. "You going to light the fuse?"

Bowen lit it. They went back to the draw to wait for the explosion and Bowen watched Brazil. The gunman squinted, his mouth open and tensed, waiting, and he seemed to be smiling, keenly anticipating what was to come.

And when it came, more suddenly than they could be ready for it, the rock-shattering, head-numbing violence, the thunder rolling into the distance, somewhere beyond the ringing in their ears, Brazil still smiled.

"Damn!" He shook his head slowly as if the pleasure of it had exhausted him. "I'd like to see what would happen to a man sitting on one of them."

"You never know," Pryde said. "Maybe you will."

Brazil looked at him. "Did you see anybody get blowed up at Yuma?"

"Not me," Pryde said.

"Did you?" Brazil asked Bowen.

Bowen shook his head.

Brazil seemed disappointed. "Maybe somebody got it before you were there. Didn't you hear of anybody?"

"I wasn't listening," Bowen said.

Brazil grinned. "That would be some sight."

They went down to the shelf again as Renda and a guard brought up the convicts to do the grading. Bowen looked over the edge. There were still two guards down in the canyon. So he's got another man on, Bowen thought. One of the night guards.

"That one took more slope," Renda said. "They hardly got any chipping off to do."

"We tried a bigger charge," Bowen told him. "Packing more sticks to the bundle."

"You go any bigger, we'll be filling in," Renda said. His gaze moved along the edge of the shelf, then stopped. Unexpectedly, Bowen saw his face become tensed. He followed Renda's gaze up canyon and saw a rider moving along the stretch of new road. Now all of them were watching and soon they saw that it was Lizann Falvey.

Brazil said, "What's she doing up here?"

Renda continued to watch her, his eyes half closed in the sun glare. A swirl of wind blew dust at him, fanning his hatbrim, but he did not turn away from it.

"I never saw her up this far," Brazil said.

She bothers him, Bowen thought, still watching Renda. All she has to do is show herself and he's on his guard. You thought it once. Maybe she's threatening him. Confident

116

she's leaving and she throws it in his face. Tells him everything but *how*.

Following Lizann, trailing her perhaps fifty yards, was a Mimbreño. Bowen watched him move off to the east side of the canyon. Lizann had circled and now was riding back toward him, past him, becoming smaller, and soon she was out of sight. But even after she was gone, Renda continued to stare up canyon and a moment later he moved down the shelf.

That's good, Bowen thought. Give him something else to think about.

Bowen indicated where the next charge would be placed before they moved back up onto the rim. And now they got ready the fuses and the dynamite cartridges they would use.

"I think I'll light the next one," Brazil said.

"That's all you got to do," Bowen said, "and you're a dynamite man."

Brazil was studying his Winchester. "It's a far size bigger than this."

Bowen looked toward Manring and nodded. Manring rose, picking up his shovel and started for the draw.

Brazil's head came up. "They're not ready for you yet."

"Earl's got another job," Bowen said. He rose as Brazil did and walked over to the edge of the draw. "He's going to dig that corner where we tested yesterday."

Brazil frowned. "What for?"

"After a couple of more blasts," Bowen explained, "we'll be far enough down to come back to the part we skipped. Earl thought he'd get it ready now if it's all right with you."

"Frank know about it?"

"Ask him," Bowen said. He turned and walked back to Pryde.

Brazil glanced at Manring. "Go on. I'll see him later." He squatted then at the edge of the draw where he could watch Bowen and Pryde, to his left, and Manring below and to his right.

"The first step," Pryde murmured.

Bowen sat down with his back to Brazil. The detonator boxes were in front of him. He raised one box, then another, and raising the third one he felt the weight of the

117

Colt revolver. He lined up the boxes and placed this one on the right.

Now he studied the dark mass of pines that were forty or fifty yards in front of him and he began setting a fuse into the open end of a detonator.

"Ike, have you seen Mimbres?"

"For about a hair of a minute. When we first came up."

"We have to figure six on this side," Bowen said. "They don't like what's going on, so they stay back in the trees."

"What would we do if they didn't mind it?"

"Think of something else."

"And six more on the other side of the canyon," Pryde said.

"We'll think of them when the time comes," Bowen said. He crimped the open end of the detonator to the fuse. He unwrapped one end of the dynamite cartridge, pushed a twig into it to form an opening, then inserted a detonator.

"How many you going to do?" Pryde asked.

"We'll have five ready," Bowen said. "Maybe we won't use that many, but we'll have them."

"Brazil wants to light the fuse," Pryde said. "It'd be purely simple to leave him with it."

"Don't even think about it."

"I can't help it. It's too good not to."

"Ike, we do it the way I said."

"I know it. I was just talking."

Bowen had attached the fuse to the fourth detonator and was inserting it into the cartridge when Brazil called to him. "Earl says he's ready."

Rising, Bowen said to Pryde, "Like he works for us." He picked up a coil of fuse and a detonator and moved down the draw. Pryde followed, a half-full case of dynamite on his shoulder.

Brazil said, "What're you in such a hurry to plant this one for?"

Bowen dropped the coil, but held an end of it. "Might as well do it now as later."

"You sure Frank knows about it?"

"Go ask him," Bowen said. He saw Brazil's gaze go down into the canyon.

"Frank would've told me," Brazil said.

"He tells you everything?"

118

Brazil did not answer. He was studying the small figures far below. He said then, "I don't see him."

Now the four of them looked down into the canyon. Almost at once Pryde said, "That's him . . . riding off. Way up the road there."

"Like he's going back to camp," Manring said. He looked at Brazil. "Everybody works but Frank."

"You dig your hole," Brazil snapped. "And keep your mouth shut."

"It's dug."

"Then plant the charge!"

That's it, Bowen thought. Get mad. Get your mind on something else.

When they climbed out of the draw again, a ten-foot length of fuse hung curling to the ground from the hole where the charge was buried. The hole had been dug above the undercut of their test blast of the previous day. It was approximately five feet from the ground.

"When you going to light it?" Brazil asked Bowen.

"I figure sometime this afternoon."

Brazil's gaze found the four dynamite sticks with fuses already attached. "You're doing a damn awful lot of work beforehand."

"What difference does it make when we do it? Long as it gets done."

"Maybe I ought to ask you that," Brazil said.

Bowen shrugged. "Pull the detonators out if you don't want them there. We'll walk off about a half mile and watch you."

Bowen turned from him. He went over to the equipment, sat down next to Pryde and began fitting a fuse end into the fifth detonator, thinking, now watching Brazil wander to the edge of the draw: Don't push him too far.

Manring stooped next to Bowen. "Are we ready?"

"As ready as we'll ever be."

"How much did you plant just now?"

"Twenty pounds."

"Is that enough?"

"I'd have set more if it wasn't."

"We got to be sure."

"What do you want to do," Bowen said, "light it now and find out?"

Manring's hand scratched nervously at his beard. "We got to be sure, that's all."

Pryde got to his feet. They saw him stare off toward the pass that was beyond the end of the canyon. Then Brazil noticed him, hearing the hoof sounds at the same time. "Sit down," he told Pryde, and swung the Winchester toward the pass.

As he did, Karla Demery appeared in the shadowed opening. She looked up, showing surprise at seeing them, then walked her horse toward them.

Her gaze moved from Bowen and the two men next to him to Brazil. "I didn't think you'd be up here so soon."

"We're full of surprises," Brazil grinned. He saw her move to dismount. "Sit where you are. I got enough to watch without a horse standing by."

"I wanted to see if these men had any letters," Karla said. Her hand was behind her on the saddlebag, unfastening the strap.

"Give them to Frank," Brazil said.

"It'll only take a minute." Karla brought out the letters, began going through them, then glanced at Bowen again. "Isn't your name Bowen?"

Bowen nodded. His eyes moved to Brazil. Brazil was watching Karla.

"I thought I had a letter for you," Karla said. She came to the last letter, then started through them again. "It seems to me it was from an attorney. The return address, I mean. Lyall Martz? Is that name familiar to you?"

"Yes, ma'am," Bowen said.

"But now I don't see it."

Brazil moved toward them. "What would you be hearing from a lawyer about?"

"He's a friend," Bowen said.

Karla looked up. "I know there was a letter from him. Somehow I must have misplaced it. Tomorrow . . . I'll be sure to bring it tomorrow."

"He can wait," Brazil said. "Now move out of here."

"I remember it looked like such an important letter," Karla said.

Brazil's hand came down on the horse's rump and it sidestepped away from him. Karla looked back, then reined toward the draw and Brazil called after her, "When you find Frank, tell him I want to see him!"

Manring leaned toward Bowen. "What's this lawyer business?"

"You think it concerns you?"

"We were in it together, weren't we?"

"You don't fit into it, Earl," Bowen murmured. He began taking dynamite cartridges from an open case and binding them into bundles of eight sticks.

And you don't fit into it either, he told himself. You don't hang on to a thread. Not now. Maybe when there was time, but now it's a matter of minutes. You understand that? Minutes.

A convict appeared out of the draw and told Manring the charge hole was ready to be dug. He stood with hands on hips looking about idly, to the pass, up into the trees, then his eyes dropped to Bowen who was winding twine about the dynamite sticks and he moved back down the draw. Manring followed him.

Watching him go, Pryde murmured, "We could leave Earl there too."

"All four of us walk back up here," Bowen said.

"How're you going to handle Brazil?"

Bowen glanced over his shoulder—Brazil was still at the edge of the draw—then raised the top from the detonator box which held the revolver. "Like this."

"Where'd you get that?"

"I'm not saying."

"I could guess."

"And you'd be wrong." Bowen closed the box.

"You going to shoot Brazil?"

Bowen shook his head.

"Let me have it," Pryde said. "I'll use it on him."

"You got enough to do," Bowen said; then asked, "Have you got it straight?"

"I think so."

"Tell it."

Pryde's eyes raised to Brazil, then lowered again. "When we're called to set the charge, you're going first. You carry the case with the bundles in it. Then I follow. I'm carrying another case. There're a few sticks in it and the knife. You get down to the end of the draw before you notice I'm carrying it. Then you say, 'I got enough sticks. Leave what you got here and we'll pick it up on the way back.' I set the case down where you planted the charge a while ago. Right under where the fuse is hanging. Then we go around on the trail and do what we're supposed to be doing. You light the charge and we all hurry back up the trail. We're starting up the draw and I say that I've forgot the case. I lag back to get it, take the knife out of the case, cut the fuse so only five feet is hanging out of the wall, light it and come after you."

"That gives you a minute and a half," Bowen said, "to climb out of the draw."

"It doesn't take half of that," Pryde said.

"You want to be on the safe side."

"But why a five-foot fuse?"

"We want this charge to go off as close as possible with the main one," Bowen said. "If they blow too far apart, somebody down below will start to think about it and come up too soon to find out why. But we couldn't put on just five feet when we planted the charge, because Brazil would notice it being short and wonder about it."

"But with the draw caved in," Pryde said, "nobody could get up here anyway."

"This way is called not leaving anything to chance," Bowen said. "Maybe there's a quick way up out of the canyon we don't even know about."

"All right." Pryde nodded, then asked, "When do you pull the gun?"

"As soon as the draw blows," Bowen said. "Whether it goes before or after or at the same time the main charge does, Brazil won't expect it. He'll be off guard."

"Then we tie him up," Pryde said.

"That's right." Bowen glanced at the row of long-fused dynamite cartridges next to him. "While Earl cuts the fuses on those."

"Why don't we do it now?"

"For the same reason that charge down in the draw has a ten-foot fuse," Bowen said. "Brazil isn't that dumb. If he sees six-inch fuses sticking out of these he'll know damn well what they're for."

"And the rest is up to luck," Pryde said.

Bowen shrugged. "Maybe we'll make our own."

The convict who had come for Manring a few minutes before appeared again at the top of the draw.

"Here we go," Pryde said.

Brazil looked toward them and called, "Ready for the stuff."

Rising, lifting the case to his shoulder, Bowen said, "Take your time. Cut the fuse right where it touches the ground and you'll have five feet."

Pryde nodded. "Don't worry about it." As Bowen walked off, he picked up the second wooden case and followed him. Brazil fell in behind going down the draw. No one spoke and there was only the sound of their steps in the loose gravel. Then, as they reached the shelf, Bowen looked back.

"Ike, what've you got that for?"

Pryde stopped. "Didn't you say bring it?

"I got all we need," Bowen said. "Set it down there and we'll pick it up on the way back." His eyes moved to Brazil. No reaction. No change in his tight-jawed, narrow-eyed expression.

Bowen turned the corner and moved down the shelf, along the thirty feet which they had not yet dynamited, then over the widened, graded section—roughly fifty feet of this—to the place where they would set off the next blast.

Manring was waiting there. The grading crew had moved out and were already at the bottom of the trail. "Ready?" asked Manring.

Bowen only nodded. He stepped into the closet-sized space that had been cut into the wall and began placing the charges. The horizontal chamber that Manring had prepared was waist high and ran parallel with the wall of the canyon. It was deep enough to hold all of the charges, but it was too wide; and with each charge that he placed Bowen would tamp sand into the chamber so the dynamite would fit snugly and there would be no air space. When he finished, only the fuse could be seen extending from the packed sand.

Bowen looked at Brazil. "You said you wanted to light it."

"I'll hold your rifle," Pryde said.

"I guess you would," Brazil said. He waved the barrel of the Winchester. "You all get out of the way. Start moving up." He drew a match and stooped over the fuse, then called after the three men, "This one's ten feet?"

Bowen turned and nodded. "Three minutes' worth." He

watched Brazil strike the match and hold it to the fuse. "Give him room," Bowen murmured.

He turned again, now hearing Brazil coming up behind them, and started to walk faster.

Brazil called, "What's the hurry?"

Bowen glanced back. "That one's bigger than the others. We got to get all the way up to the top."

Pryde let Bowen pass him. He was next to Brazil as they turned into the draw. Then he stopped. And as Brazil went on, Bowen and Manring ahead of him, he stooped quickly, took the knife from the wooden case and cut the fuse so that less than a foot of it remained. Bowen looked back as he brought the knife down.

"What's the matter?" Bowen called.

Brazil stopped.

Pryde stepped in front of the cut-off fuse and waved up to Bowen, the knife palmed in his other hand. "Go on. I got to get this box is all." He watched Bowen and Manring move up through the draw. Brazil turned to follow them.

"Hey!" Pryde called sharply, bringing Brazil around. He waited. Brazil frowned. Now Bowen and Manring were reaching the top of the draw. Pryde waited a moment longer, until they were over the rim. Then he said, "Come here."

Brazil started toward him, but stopped, as if only then remembering the burning fuse down on the trail. "Pick it up . . . we got to *move!*"

Pryde stared at him. "You're not going anywhere."

"What'd you say?"

"You heard me."

Brazil's gaze went beyond Pryde and abruptly his eyes opened wide. "What'd you do to that fuse!"

Something was wrong. Something was going on that shouldn't be happening. But even as he realized it, even as his nerves came alive and he reflexively brought up the Winchester, it was too late, Pryde was on him.

He tried to go back, tried to level the Winchester, but Pryde's left hand pushed up on the barrel. Brazil's arms went up with it and he half turned to wrench the Winchester from Pryde's grasp. As he did, Pryde's right hand drove the knife into his side. Brazil gasped and the shock of it was in his eyes and in his straining, open-mouthed expression as he slumped to the ground.

Pryde was at the fuse again. He struck a match, touched it to the fuse and started to run. A ten-inch fuse—time enough to climb out of the draw, but not for Bowen to come down after Brazil. You had to think of Bowen doing things like that.

He was twenty feet from the rim when the main charge went off and the suddenness of it made him stumble. His ears rang and there was dust in the air and the echo up canyon and suddenly Pryde fell again.

His hands clutched at his stomach. He felt a wetness and looking down saw that it was his own blood. He could not believe it, but it was there. He had been shot and the bullet had gone completely through him. But there had been no report! Only the ringing and the echo and the slamming against his back that could have been a rock—

He rolled over and felt himself sliding and then he saw Brazil at the bottom of the draw. He was lying on his stomach aiming the Winchester.

"Ike!"—above him, Bowen's voice.

Pryde saw the Winchester raise and he called out to warn Bowen.

FOURTEEN

BOWEN had already seen Brazil. He went down, rolling away from the slope, hearing Pryde's one-word scream lost in the high-whining, dust-kicking report of the Winchester.

There was no time to think, yet it was in his mind to help Pryde. He had returned to the defile in time to see only part of it—Pryde lighting the fuse and running, Brazil rolling to his stomach, bringing up the Winchester, then the blast going off down on the shelf and Pryde stumbling—

And now, even knowing it was too late, Bowen thought of Lizann's revolver. He pushed up to his hands and knees, then was moving, running for the row of detonator boxes when the draw erupted behind him.

The force of it slammed him to the ground and he covered his head with his arms as the sand and rock fragments showered down on him. Then he was up again, the hissing ringing of the explosion still tight about him, seeing Manring coming toward him, Manring looking past him to where the draw had been.

The left wall of the draw had been blown in, completely filling the narrow depression, so that now a steep slope of shattered rock dropped to the shelf and covered the section of it that had curved into the draw.

"Ike's under there," Bowen murmured. "He cut the fuse short, tried to leave Brazil there, but Brazil shot him—"

Manring looked back toward the trees. What had happened to Pryde meant nothing—not with Mimbres about to appear. He said urgently, "We got to move!" and started back toward the equipment.

Bowen stared down the slope. Was it worth that? You didn't do it—it was his own fault!

"Come on!" Manring's voice.

Bowen's gaze went down into the canyon. He saw the convicts, small figures far below, and a rider moving up canyon. He turned and ran toward Manring. "Cut the fuses!"

"With what?" Manring looked at him helplessly. "Ike

126

had the knife!" He turned to the trees nervously. "With what, damn it!"

"We'll cut them," Bowen said. "Hold on to yourself."

"We got to get out of here!"

Bowen's eyes went over the equipment. No knife...but the hand axe.

He picked it up, gathered the five dynamite sticks he had prepared and had lined up on the ground, ran his hand down all five fuses at once, drawing them together, then chopped down with the hatchet—once, twice, again, until he had chopped through all of them and only eight inches of fuse remained with each cartridge.

"There!" Manring was still looking at the trees. "I saw one!"

Bowen looked up. Off through the trees he could see a movement. Now you have to be careful, he thought. Not too close.

He struck a match, held it to a fuse, then picked up the stick and threw it. The dynamite exploded as it struck the ground ten yards out from the trees.

He told Manring, "When I throw the next one, run. And he thought: You don't even have to light it. But it's better to be sure.

He struck a match, touched it to a fuse and threw the stick in the same direction. It was end over end in the air as Manring started to run, striking the ground and exploding as Bowen took the revolver from the detonator box and shoved it inside his shirt and into his waist. He picked up the three remaining cartridges and ran after Manring.

They ran for the pass that wound through the rocks beyond the end of the canyon, followed its narrow, shadowed course and as they came out Bowen lighted and dropped another stick. They were running down the length of the meadow when it exploded behind them.

Now the Mimbres from the other side, Bowen told himself. He turned to stand in the open, in the thick grama grass that moved in slow waves with the wind.

Manring turned, hesitating. "Come on!"

Bowen motioned to him to go on. "I'll catch up." He turned back to face the rocks, hearing Manring moving through the tall grass, the hurried swishing sound becoming fainter. This is something, he thought. Covering for him. No, you're covering for yourself too. This is the way to do it. It's a once-and-for-all thing. If it works. If they scare easy.

He saw them then—the six riders slightly off to the right coming down through the rocks. They had seen him, he was sure of that, and now they had reached the meadow and were coming directly for him.

You can spot them by the way they ride, Bowen thought. Straight on and no games this time. All business.

He struck a match with his thumbnail, held it as he judged the distance closing between him and the Mimbres, then touched it to the dynamite and threw the stick.

It struck and exploded twenty yards in front of the Mimbres, and they swerved right and left. They started circling back out of range and Bowen threw the last stick, arching it higher into the air. It exploded closer than the first one and the next moment they were galloping back up the slope, winding through the rock formations.

Bowen ran on through the meadow, came out of it and started up the slope ahead of him. Near the wagon road that skirted the shoulder of the hill, he caught up with Manring.

"Now Pinaleño," Bowen said.

Frank Renda had descended the five-shadowed grade and was approaching the camp when the main charge went off in the canyon. He heard it faintly in the distance and in his mind saw a section of wall high above the shelf buckle out, seem to rise and hang suspended, then disappear into thick dust—as the previous blasts had appeared from the floor of the canyon.

But he pictured this for only a moment. His thoughts returned to Lizann Falvey. She was the business at hand. Something to be dealt with *now*. You let a woman get a little bit sure of herself and pretty soon she makes you sick to your stomach watching her pretend she's a man. Lizann had gone far enough. Riding into the canyon had been, in fact, too far.

He had forbidden her ever to come near the road construction. "Ride anywhere you want, but stay away from the convicts when you got a horse." That meant stay out of the canyon. But this morning she had come down the new road—telling him without words what she thought of his authority.

Maybe she was bluffing. Maybe she was only trying to worry him. But she seemed too sure of herself. Maybe she did have a plan. Whichever it was, he intended to find out now.

There was no guard at the gate. He had shifted one of the night men to day work when the dynamiting began. Why, he was not sure; but it seemed to him there should be another guard on hand while they were working with high explosives.

The night man was sleeping now and the gate was open. As Renda passed into the compound, the sound of the second explosion reached him. He reined in abruptly and sat listening.

An echo?

That's all. He relaxed, nudging the big chestnut to a walk, thinking: Brazil's there. He'll shoot if anybody even looks at him sideways.

He dismounted in front of the Falveys' quarters and entered the open doorway without knocking. As he did, Lizann came out of the bedroom. She had changed from her riding suit and was fastening the top buttons of her dress. She showed no surprise at seeing Renda.

"What do you want now?"

"I saw you in the canyon a while ago."

"You rode all the way in to tell me that?"

"I told you never to go near there."

She nodded. "Three or four times."

"I'm not going to tell you again."

"That's fine."

"Next time you go in the punishment cell."

"You wouldn't dare."

"You want to find out, go ahead."

Lizann smiled faintly. "Frank, do you honestly think you're frightening me?"

"If I'm not, you're the one's going to suffer for it."

"I don't think so," Lizann said. She moved across the room to the table, poured water into a glass from an earthenware pitcher, then sat down. She crossed her legs, sitting sideways to the table and sipped at the glass. "Frank," she said, lowering the glass, "I'd ask you to stay, but I

129

couldn't think of anything more unpleasant to have happen."

Renda moved toward her. "Lizzy, you're bluffing, aren't you."

"About you being unpleasant?"

"About leaving here."

A smile touched Lizann's mouth. "Why do you think I'm bluffing?"

"Because you know what I'd do to you if you ever tried."

"Has it kept you awake—thinking about it?"

"If you're not bluffing, Lizzy, you'll wish you were."

"Frank, stop trying to sound menacing. You don't frighten me anymore. I'm leaving here . . . there's nothing you can do about it, and the sooner you realize it the better."

He moved to the table, raised his hip to sit on the edge and folded his arms. Looking down at her he asked, "How're you going to do it?"

Lizann took a sip of water and placed the glass down carefully. She had expected him to show his temper, but he remained calm, deliberately in control of himself. After a moment she answered, "You'd never guess."

"I don't have to," Renda said. "You're going to tell me."

"I'll tell you this, Frank—which I already have—it's going to happen and you'll still be thinking about it when it does."

Renda watched her. As she raised the glass again, his arms uncoiled and he swept it from her hand. The glass shattered against the floor and Lizann went back from the table, straightening, looking suddenly at Renda with shocked surprise.

Renda's arms were folded again. "I asked you how're you going to do it."

Lizann did not answer, though she continued to stare at him and her hand brushed at the wet stain on her skirt.

"Willis didn't write to anybody," Renda said. "You haven't either, because I've seen every letter that's gone out. What other way is there?"

"You'll have to find out for yourself," Lizann said. She saw his arms separating and tried to turn away, but she was not quick enough and the back of his hand stung across her cheek.

As she looked up at him again, Renda said, "I'm going to find out, but not by myself. You see what I mean?"

She could feel her cheek burning as she made herself return his stare. "You intend to force me to tell you?"

Renda shrugged. "One way or the other."

"You're not a man...you're an animal."

"I'm still asking—"

"You can go to hell."

She was expecting it, but his hand struck so suddenly there was not time to turn from the blow, and as her head came up he struck her again with his open right hand.

"I'm not fooling, Lizzy!"

She brought her arms up in front of her and as he drew back his hand again she left the chair. Renda was on her as she reached the bedroom door. He pushed her inside and against the near wall, held her against the adobe until she stopped struggling, then stepped back slowly.

"The next time I use my fist!"

"I told you—"

He brought his fist back, but at the last moment he opened it and struck her again with the palm of his hand.

"Say it!"

"I have nothing to say."

Renda stepped back. He shifted his weight and saw her eyes close as he hit her in the face with his fist. Lizann's head struck the wall and she started to go down, but Renda caught her and held her against the adobe.

"I'll bust your face wide open. Honest to God I'll fix you so no man'll look at you as long as you live."

Lizann's eyes opened. She breathed in and out slowly, painfully, and said, "Let me sit down...I'll tell you."

"You're stalling."

"Let me sit down—"

Renda held her against the wall. "How're you going to do it?"

"Willis wrote a letter. He mailed it from Fuegos."

"You're lying!"

"I swear it's the truth!"

Renda went back a half step and drove his fist against her cheek.

"I'll kill you! You understand that!" He moved against her before she could slide to the floor. Close to her face he said, "One more will fix you. One more and even Willis won't know you." Her head hung forward, resting on his

131

shoulder. He could feel her breathing against him, but she made no sign that she had heard.

"All right," Renda said. His left hand held her against the wall as he stepped back.

Lizann raised her head. The side of her face was deep red, her cheekbone was skinned and a thin line of blood showed at the corner of her eye. Her eyes remained closed as she said, "I wrote the letter."

"You're lying!"

"I did!"

"How could you mail it?"

"I gave it to that girl from the station." That was it. It was forming in her mind now—something to make him leave, something to give her time—but the pain made it difficult to think and she knew she had to be careful. You gave it to the girl, she thought hurriedly. But she hasn't mailed it yet. He must think he can still get it. But get him out—for God's sake get him out!

"When did you give it to her?"

Lizann opened her eyes slowly. "She was here just before you came. A few minutes before."

"Nobody passed me. Not a soul."

"Then she came the other way. I don't know . . . but I gave it to her."

"Lizzy, if you're lying to me—"

"I swear it!"

Suddenly Renda turned from her. There was the sound of a horse outside. He waited. "Stay where you are," he said then and went out into the front room. The moment he reached the doorway he saw that his horse was gone. He ran out, hearing the running hoofbeats now—two horses, one of them his, both moving through the open gate, then swinging south toward the wagon road.

"Karla!" Renda cupped his hands to his mouth and shouted after her. She did not look back, but he saw her release his horse before she disappeared over a low-swelling rise.

Lizann stood in the doorway to the bedroom. "What did you say? You called something."

"Karla . . . she was still here."

"You're sure?"

"Listening to us all the time," Renda said. "Else she wouldn't be running now."

Lizann stared at him.

"Now I'll have to go after her," Renda said. He looked at Lizann again. "I would've sworn you were lying. You're lucky she was still around. You know I just might have killed you."

Lizann nodded slowly. She did not trust herself to speak.

FIFTEEN

THEY HAD COME down the wagon-road slope keeping in line with the windowless north side of the stage station and now, from the willows, they looked across the open yard to the front of the adobe.

"One horse in the shed," Manring said.

Bowen was studying it. From this angle they could see only the hindquarters and saddle. "It could be Willis Falvey's dun," Bowen said. Karla wouldn't be back yet, he thought. That left her father and whoever owned the dun. That you're sure of, he thought.

"It could be," Manring said. "That'd be something if he was inside."

Bowen's hand went into the front of his shirt. "We're about to find out," he said. As he pulled Lizann's revolver he saw the look of surprise come over Manring's bearded face.

"Where'd you get that?"

"I told you, Earl, we didn't need you as much as you thought." Bowen turned and as Manring continued to stare at him, moved out from the willows.

He started to hurry across the open yard, then thought: Take your time. He slowed to a walk, keeping his eyes on the door, but not going directly for it. He reached the corner of the building, hesitated, then moved along the front of the adobe, past the two windows, to the screen door. He opened it, felt it open wider as Manring took it, and brought up the revolver as he stepped into the room.

At the far end, behind the bar, John Demery looked up. As he did, as the astonishment came over his face, Willis Falvey glanced around, then turned suddenly, pressing his back to the bar.

Bowen said. "Who else is here?" moving toward them.

Demery shook his head. "Nobody else. Karla—" he stopped. "You broke out!"

Bowen motioned with the revolver. "Come around to this side." He glanced at Manring. "Look out back."

134

Manring was staring at Falvey. "I got to talk to little Willis." He walked toward him, ignoring Bowen.

Falvey pressed against the bar. "I never did anything to you."

"Leave him alone," Bowen said.

Falvey looked toward Bowen. "I don't even know his name. How could I have done anything to him?"

Close to him Manring said, "You were there, boy. That's enough."

Bowen stepped toward them. "Get away from him, Earl." Falvey's face was flushed; he'd had a lot of whisky, Bowen judged, but not enough to hide his open-eyed, lip-biting expression of fear.

"I don't care if you run away," Falvey said. "More power to you. Ask John here, I was telling him...I don't care anymore what goes on at that place."

"He doesn't care," Demery said. "But not enough to pull out."

Falvey turned on him. "Why should I? I do my job! What Frank does is none of my business!" He caught himself then. "You don't even know what you're talking about."

"You're doing the talking," Demery said. "Maybe I don't know everything; but living within six miles of that place, and watching you, I know enough."

Abruptly, Manring pulled Falvey around by his coat lapels. "Willis, are you packing a gun?"

Falvey shook his head emphatically. "It's on my saddle. Gun and holster both hanging on the saddle."

Manring released him, stepping back. "Let's see."

Falvey's hands went to his coat. He unbuttoned it and was holding it open when Manring's fist drove into his face. Head and shoulders snapped back and as his knees buckled Manring hit him again.

"Leave him alone!" Bowen was on Manring pushing him away and Demery caught Falvey before he could fall.

Manring stepped back, looking at Bowen now. "You're a real do-gooder, aren't you?"

"Earl, get out of here. Take a look out back; then bring the dun around and saddle another horse."

"So you're bossing," Manring said mildly.

Bowen nodded. "Now you're sure of it."

"That's a lot of order giving," Manring said, "for a man who's still got numbers on his pants."

Bowen moved the revolver toward him. "You're on a poor end for arguing about it, Earl." He held the revolver on him until Manring turned and went out through the kitchen.

To Falvey, Bowen said, "You'd better sit down."

Falvey shook his head. "I'm all right." He took out a handkerchief to wipe the blood from his mouth, then turned to the bar and drank down the whisky still in his glass.

Demery watched Bowen move to one of the front windows. "You didn't see Karla," he said. "You couldn't have."

Looking out across the yard to the willows Bowen said, "I saw her. She passed us just before . . . just before we ran off."

"I mean," Demery said, "you didn't *talk* to her."

Bowen looked at him now. "She wanted to tell me something, but Brazil was there." It seemed a long time ago and he had almost forgotten it.

"Well, it doesn't matter now," Demery said.

"What doesn't?"

"Man, you got a new trial coming up. New evidence, new trial, new everything!"

"What—"

"You heard me right—a new trial! With about an eighty per cent chance of going free. But you have to break out and ruin any chance you ever had!"

Bowen stared at him. "How do you know?"

"We heard from Lyall Martz."

"Karla didn't tell me anything about a new trial! How was I to know—"

"She told you about the lawyer!"

"That was talk."

"Talk!" Demery said hotly. "Those two have been working for you for a month—Karla pleading at Lyall and Lyall pulling more strings than a four-team driver. And all the time you're thinking how to do it the hard way. You couldn't wait. Got to bust out with your bare hand as if that would prove something." Demery moved around the end of the bar. He poured whisky into a glass and pushed it at Bowen. "Have a drink."

Bowen exhaled slowly. He raised the glass and drank off the whisky. He tried to smile then. "I guess my timing's poor."

"I guess it is," Demery said. He hesitated before adding, "But maybe not so poor to be too late."

"What do you mean?"

Demery looked at Falvey. "Willis, if this man gives himself up, will you look after him, be responsible for him till a marshal comes from Prescott?"

Falvey hesitated. "I don't see how I could."

"You could stay right here. We'll lock him in a room and you could stand right there at the bar till the Prescott man comes."

"I don't have the authority—"

"Damn it, take the authority!"

Falvey shook his head. "It's out of my jurisdiction."

"Willis, the man just saved you from getting your head beat in!"

"I'm sorry—"

Demery shook his head. "He's sorry."

Bowen placed his elbows on the bar, leaning toward Demery. "What'd the lawyer find out, Mr. Demery?"

"All the things that should've come out at the trial," the station agent said. "Lyall found the man who'd forged the cattleman's name on the bill of sale."

"Then Earl didn't do it."

"No," Demery said. "He didn't do it. He paid to have it done."

"You're sure."

"Of course I'm sure. This forger's name is Roy Avery. He confessed to his part and told everything he knew."

Bowen shook his head. "I never heard of him."

"Avery says he never heard of you either," Demery said. "He signed a statement that it was his understanding Manring was in it alone. He said you must've been hired just as a hand."

"How'd the lawyer get Avery to make the statement?" asked Bowen.

"Lyall's full of tricks," Demery said. "But he might've just held a gun on him for all I know."

"I'm obliged to him."

"You sure as hell are." Demery paused before saying, "That's some partner you've got. Takes you to jail with him."

"I don't call him a partner."

"But you break out together."

"That's a long story."

"I bet it is."

"Listen," Bowen said, "till Karla started this, Earl was innocent as far as I knew. I was mad because he got me into it, but after a while I thought: If you have to live with him then you might as well make the best of it. I never cared for his ways, but I never had cause to doubt him till Karla talked to the lawyer."

"But after she talked to him," Demery said, "and told you about it, you still teamed with him to break out."

"When you're behind the fence," Bowen said, "you don't think the same as when you're outside. A chance comes to run, you take it—even if you have doubts about the man you're running with."

"But no doubts now?"

"I guess not."

Demery said, "I still don't know why he didn't clear you at the trial. He didn't gain anything by your going to prison."

Bowen shook his head. "I don't know either. But we're going to find out."

"Knowing won't do you any good," Demery said, "unless you get out of here before Renda comes."

"No, Mr. Demery, I don't think I'll leave now."

"Frank won't accept this lawyer thing. He'll think up an excuse to shoot you."

"I'll take a chance."

"What about the Mimbres?"

"Damn—everything at once."

"You got a lot to think about."

"But you take the important one first, don't you?"

"That's what they say."

"And that's Earl. Earl's not leaving either."

As Bowen said this, he heard the back screen door slam and he stepped around the end of the bar to be facing the doorway. Lizann's revolver was in front of him on the bar. Manring's steps sounded from the kitchen, then he was in the doorway, standing hip-cocked and wearing Willis Falvey's Colt.

"You coming?"

"We're not going anywhere, Earl."

"What's that supposed to mean?"

Get to it, Bowen thought, and he said, "Your friend Avery made a statement."

Manring straightened slowly, letting his hands slide from his hips. "Are you talking to me?"

"You know I am."

"I don't know any Avery. Avery what?"

"You'll meet him again at the trial."

"Somebody's been fooling you, boy." Manring's eyes went to Demery. "What's he been making up?"

Bowen raised his elbows to the bar. "Unstrap the gun, Earl, and we won't have to talk so much."

"What's he been telling you?"

"I already said it. Avery made a statement and there's going to be a new trial. You're going to be there to tell it in your own words."

Manring shook his head. "Corey, a man can talk you into just about anything, can't he?"

"I guess he can."

"A real honest-to-God do-gooder."

"You better start unbuckling the belt."

"Corey, don't you see what he's done?" Manring shook his head again and a faint smile showed in his beard. "He's made up that story to stall us. He figured how to get to you right away and made up this story about a new trial. We already had one. They don't try a man twice. Don't you know that? A man can't be tried twice for the same crime. That's a *law*."

Demery said, "There's a pile of poor reasoning going on in this room."

Manring's hands moved to his hips again as he glanced at Demery. "If I was in your shoes I'd quit pushing it."

Watch him, Bowen thought. Every move. Briefly his eyes dropped to the revolver on the bar. Looking up again, its position was in his mind and he knew where his hand would go if it had to.

"Corey," Manring said. "There's a reward for helping bring back escaped convicts. That's what the old man is thinking about. It's worth making up a story for."

"Earl, why didn't you tell at the trial I was innocent?"

"I did! We both were."

"You know what I mean."

Manring shook his head wearily. "If you're going to keep talking like that, I'm going on by myself."

"You're not going anywhere."

Manring paused, staring at Bowen. "I'm walking out, Corey. If you want to stop me, you'll have to shoot me in the back."

Bowen said nothing.

"Corey, I don't have any fight against you. Even right now." Manring's voice was quiet and seemed edged with disappointment. "But I can't stand here and listen to any more. If you want to stay, all right. Then we'll part company right now."

His eyes dropped and he turned to walk through the doorway, but he stopped in the middle of his stride with the unmistakable sound of a hammer being cocked—a thin, metallic *click,* and after that, silence.

Facing the doorway, Manring didn't move. Then, slowly, in the silence, he seemed to relax and he said, "All right, Corey." He turned carefully, then shook his head seeing the revolver leveled at him. "Now what're you doing that for?" He started toward Bowen. "Put the gun down, Corey. We'll talk it over—get everything out in the open."

"Unfasten the gun belt," Bowen said. "Let it drop."

Manring came on. Reaching the bar, he said, "For a minute there, Corey, you scared hell out of me. I almost thought you were going to shoot." His left hand brought the whisky bottle toward him and he glanced at Bowen. "You want one?"

Bowen shook his head. *His hand on the bottle*—he was thinking it, expecting what was to happen, the next moment going to his left away from the end of the bar as Manring's hand suddenly swept the whisky bottle at him, With the sound of it smashing against the wall, Manring's hand was drawing the Colt, clearing it from the holster as he pushed himself away from the bar, seeing Bowen with a hand and a knee on the floor, and at that moment Bowen fired. It was over as suddenly as it had started.

Manring dropped the Colt as he went down and rolled to his side, his hands clutched tightly to his right thigh.

Demery moved toward him, glancing at Bowen. "You're low today."

Bowen nodded. "I don't want Earl to miss the trial on my account."

They carried Manring into Demery's bedroom and placed him on the bed. Bowen moved to the doorway in line with the front windows and stood there as Demery bound Manring's leg to stop the bleeding.

"He's lucky," Demery said, "A bigger gun would've busted it."

"What about moving him?" Bowen said. "Can he travel?"

"I don't see why not," Demery said, "I'll take you to Fuegos in the wagon. Let the doctor look at him, then board the stage. We'll give Earl a stick to bite on for the bumps."

Bowen moved closer to the bed. "You hear that, Earl? You're going to trial."

Manring stared at the ceiling and said nothing.

"Earl, why didn't you tell them I was innocent?"

Manring looked at him then. "You must be awful lucky to get by as dumb as you are."

"You didn't gain by it," Bowen said. "Once you were sentenced, why didn't you explain how it was?"

"What's the difference?" Manring said. "You'd still be here."

"Is that the only reason—because they wouldn't believe you even if you told?"

"There's a real dumb do-gooder for you," Manring said. His expression changed to anger. "You forget that night before the trial!"

Puzzled, Bowen said, "In the jail cell?"

"In the cell—when you tried to beat my head in!"

"You let me get sent to Yuma for that?"

"Listen to him," Manring said. "You got what you drawed, boy. Thinking you're so damn better than anybody else—dumb as you are—you deserved to get sent away."

"Earl, that doesn't make sense."

"Well, think about it a while. In your case it takes longer to sink in."

Demery said, "I'd have aimed higher, Corey. About two feet up and a little to the left."

Manring glared at him. "You and your mouth can go to hell."

Bowen turned as Falvey appeared in the doorway. "Somebody's coming," Falvey said, and as he did they could hear hoofbeats in the yard.

Bowen moved past him, going to a front window. He saw her then, already dismounting, and heard Demery say,

"It's Karla," going out the door, the screen slamming behind him. Through the window he saw Karla running to her father. She was telling him something, but he could hear only a few of her words: Renda...and Lizann Falvey ...and Mimbres. Something about Mimbres.

He could hear their steps, the screen door opening and Karla's voice clearly now, though she was out of breath and spoke hurriedly—

"They're up on the hill—at least five or six, but I'm not sure because I came on them unexpectedly. They were all dismounted and I recognized the head one. He was there. The one who wears the hat—"

She saw Bowen then.

SIXTEEN

FROM THE PINES that crested the hill, Salvaje watched Karla
Demery ride into the willows, saw her come out the other
side and continue on at the same running pace across the
yard. As she dismounted, a man came out of the adobe and
she went to him.

The woman cannot help him, Salvaje thought in English.
She will tell we are here, but what more could she do than
that? And it matters little. Sooner or later he would come
out and find out for himself.

He thought of Bowen as he would of another Apache. He
thought of him as a man who considered carefully before
he acted. A man who did not underestimate his opponent.
And regarding Bowen this way, Salvaje had changed his
own tactics.

Instead of sending one tracker to the station to signal
the escaped man's direction, Salvaje had followed the two
men-running tracks himself all the way to these pines
which overlooked the station. Four men remained with
him. Another five were positioned in the trees which faced
the corral behind the adobe.

Perhaps they could rush the adobe and take the two men
by surprise. Perhaps the two men already knew they were
here, even before the woman came. And perhaps they still
had sticks that exploded. There were many perhapses and
one had to think carefully to outwit an opponent.

Often he thought of the time Bowen, alone, had fought
his men in the meadow and he held him in high regard.

This Bowen was a good opponent, but he seemed to not
want to cause injury and this put him at a disadvantage.
The first time he escaped, he shot at horses, but not at
men. And throwing the exploding sticks it seemed he wanted
to keep them from following, to warn them; but not to
injure or kill.

It was unfortunate that a man should be born with that
feeling; especially a man of this one's ability. But it was
also unfortunate one had to fight against him. He made it
a good fight, but it would be better to be with him than

against him. This man who took tulapai with Zele and Pindah.

But let him make the first move now. Watch this man. Perhaps one might even learn something from him. But if one did learn something—against whom would you use it? The good days were long past.

He is taking a long time, Salvaje continued to think. That could mean he is planning something worthwhile. Or perhaps the man who lives there shot him—though the sound might not have been that of a gun. Or perhaps he is afraid. No. That one could be afraid, but he would not show it by hiding.

A quarter of an hour had passed since the woman had gone down the slope. Then, as Salvaje watched the adobe, the screen door opened and a man stepped out. Salvaje rose.

He watched the man walk out a few strides, then stop, then raise his hat and wave it in the air in a slow come-forward signal. The man wore convict clothes and after only a moment of watching him Salvaje was sure that it was Bowen.

Now it begins. He wants to talk and he holds his arms up to show he is unarmed. Or he is giving himself up? No. He watched Bowen walk toward the willows.

All right, we talk. Salvaje motioned to one of his men and the two Mimbres walked down the slope side by side. They carried their Springfields and did not take their eyes from the figure of the man now standing in the deep shade of the willows. When he was almost to the trees, Salvaje motioned his man to stop and he went on alone.

Bowen stood waiting. He watched the Mimbreño part the hanging willow branches entering the shade, then stop directly across the narrow creek from him.

"You come armed," Bowen said.

"I am under no truce," the Mimbreño said. "Perhaps you should have arms yourself."

"I came to speak as a friend."

"Let me tell you something first," Salvaje said, speaking clearly, carefully. "If you beg to go free, I will shoot you before you can turn away."

"I didn't come to beg," Bowen said. "I'm going to tell you two things. If there is anything you don't understand, I ask you to take my word that it's the truth. If you don't, there's nothing I can do about it. When I'm through, it's up to you to decide what you want to do. You understand that?"

Salvaje nodded.

Quickly then, but explaining it as simply as he could, Bowen told the Mimbreño how he had been tried once for a crime he had not committed and now he was to be tried again. Briefly he explained Karla's part. Then Manring's, and what Manring had tried to do in the adobe—final proof that he was guilty.

But, Bowen explained, his own innocence would mean nothing if Renda returned him to the camp. Renda could even kill him on the way and report that he had tried to escape. He must remain free long enough to appear in court again. That was the important thing. If Salvaje did not believe this he could ask the girl in the house. She acted fairly, for hadn't Salvaje taken two of her horses yet she had not reported him?

Salvaje stared at Bowen. "But the man who is innocent kills two men in his escape."

"That was not my doing," Bowen said. "The one called Pryde tried to trap Brazil and he was killed himself."

"Will the men of the trial believe that?"

Bowen hesitated. "I don't know. I can only tell them how it happened."

"And what is the second thing?" Salvaje asked.

"The girl in the house who rode past you," Bowen said. "She had just left the camp where she saw Renda beating Falvey's woman." Bowen paused. "This is hard to explain; you see, Renda's been doing things against the law. The woman knew about it and wanted to leave, but he wouldn't let her. The girl, Karla, believes Renda is on his way here. Renda thinks the girl has a letter that will prove the unlawful things he has done." Bowen paused again. "You see, Falvey's woman, in order to get rid of him, told him the girl had been there earlier and had taken the letter with her. This was not true. As I said, it was only to make him leave. But the girl did happen to be there as they spoke. Renda saw her ride away and he believed she did have a letter."

Bowen shook his head. "Does that make sense?"

"Finish," Salvaje said.

"All right—Willis Falvey is in the house now. If he will report Renda, Renda will go to prison or even hang. Falvey is afraid of Renda, but now maybe he will report him."

"And if Renda is taken now," Salvaje said, "you will not go back to Five Shadows."

"That's right."

"And Renda will be finished."

"If we can prove what he's been doing."

"What would you have me do?" Salvaje asked.

Momentarily Bowen smiled. He said then, "Nothing."

"Nothing?"

"We have to handle this ourselves," Bowen said. "If you went against him you'd be liable for a court-martial; because nothing's been proved against him yet. But if you'll take your men away and let us handle it . . . well, I'll be grateful. It's up to you."

"You are sure of yourself," the Mimbreño said. "Or you wouldn't have come out here."

Bowen nodded. "I don't know why—I just had a feeling you'd agree."

"Perhaps we drink tulapai sometime."

Bowen nodded again. "Perhaps."

"I would like to see him finished," Salvaje said thoughtfully. "I don't understand everything, but I would like to see that happen."

"Then you'll take your men away?"

Salvaje nodded solemnly. "But wherever you are, we will be watching." He turned abruptly and moved up the slope.

Bowen walked back to the adobe. Demery waited for him in the doorway. "He's agreed," Bowen told him.

"Just like that." Demery held the door open.

Bowen paused. "You ever talk to a man who looks at you the way he does? He doesn't understand it all, but if you tried to lie he'd know it. I don't know how, but he would." Bowen stepped inside and saw Falvey standing at the bar. "What did Willis say?"

Demery shook his head. "He won't budge."

"He heard Karla tell it. What's the matter with him?"

"He says he doesn't believe us. Says we're trying to trick him into going against Renda."

Bowen saw Karla come out of Manring's room. Her eyes met his briefly, then looked away as she went into the kitchen. Bowen said quickly, "You'd think Willis'd want to go see for himself."

"That would be admitting he believes us," Demery said. "He doesn't even want to think about it. But if he moved away from that bar he'd have to."

"I don't know," Bowen said wearily. "Maybe I ought to just give myself up."

"You do," Demery told him, "and you'll never get to Prescott. You know that. This is twice you've made a fool of him. Frank will either think up a way to kill you or else bury you under so many charges nobody could get you out...The way I see it, your only chance is to get Renda before the authorities."

"If we just took him," Bowen said, "what would happen?"

"Hand him over without proof? For the same reason I didn't report some letters Frank destroyed. Letters that didn't belong to him. It would be our word against his." Demery said then, "We don't even know if he's coming."

"He'll come," Bowen said.

"He's taking his sweet time."

"Word must have reached him about the break."

"Then he won't be alone."

"His guards still have thirty men to watch. He's coming on personal business."

"If he comes."

"He'll come," Bowen said again. "If he thinks there's a letter here for Prescott, he'll come, break or no break. This is more important to him than two men running away. That's Salvaje's worry."

"He doesn't know Willis is here," Demery said. "Maybe we can make something out of that. Let's think about it."

Bowen nodded. "And the letter that's supposed to be here."

Demery nodded thoughtfully. He went to the roll-top desk, came back with an envelope and handed it to Bowen. "If you could hold a gun on Renda and tell him you've got the letter—"

"Then what?"

"I don't know. It was just a thought."

Bowen stuffed the envelope into his left pants pocket. "The holding the gun on him sounds all right...Well, we better be ready." He walked to the bar, picked up the Colt Manring had dropped and pushed it into his waist. As he did, Falvey turned from the bar. "Where did you get that gun?"

Bowen looked up questioningly. "Earl had it."

"I mean the one you used on him."

"Oh—" Bowen hesitated. "I got it out of your wife's saddlebag this morning." He watched Falvey turn to the bar again. "Frank will be here soon. You better get hold of yourself."

Falvey raised his glass. "I have no part in this."

"You can wash your hands all you want," Bowen said. "But if there's a hearing, you'll be dragged into it."

"I'll tell the authorities the same thing I'm telling you."

"They'll check your books," Bowen said. "Any man who can count will see what you've been up to."

Falvey came around as Bowen spoke. "What do you know about my books?"

"What I just said's enough."

"You don't know what you're talking about. My books are in order. There isn't a man who can prove otherwise."

"What about your wife?"

"Leave her out of it."

"Don't you want to see how she is?"

"If you think I believe that girl's story, you're out of your mind."

"Karla wouldn't lie."

"Then call it something else."

"I think you're afraid to go to your wife. When you see what's happened you'll have to do something. But you don't know what."

"Are you concerned over her?"

"Anybody would be."

Falvey turned from the bar. "The reason I ask is because she doesn't own saddlebags."

"What?"

"That you could have taken her revolver from."

"All right," Bowen said quietly. "I saw her one day in the stable and talked her into letting me have it."

"That easily?"

"It sounds simpler when you tell it."

"How would giving you a gun help her—did she say?"

Bowen shook his head. "Maybe she thought I'd use it on Renda. I don't know."

"Or on me," Falvey said. He turned back to the bar.

"Mr. Falvey, you know better than that."

"Get away from me!"

You must be easy to read, Bowen thought, remembering Salvaje but now thinking of Falvey. He walked to one of the front windows and leaned against the side frame as he looked out. No, not this time, he thought. This time you made a mistake and were caught at it and it didn't matter what your face told. He's not dumb. He knows what's going on . . . but you have to feel sorry for him, don't you?

How would you like to have a wife who wanted you killed? And you suspected it. If you didn't suspect it, at least you wouldn't put it past her. So why should he be concerned about her? You say that doesn't happen to people, but you wake up one morning and it's happening to you. No wonder he drinks. He's got a lot to drink about.

He began to think of Karla then—the look on her face as she came in and saw him in the room, almost going to him, but remembering and realizing he shouldn't be there and holding herself back. Was that it? Her father explained about the escape, but Karla didn't look at Bowen as he did, nor after, when she told about Renda and Lizann.

At first, Bowen believed she was angry—just as her father had been, because he had escaped instead of waited. Then he realized that hers was not anger at all, but indifference. At least a posed indifference. And finally he understood—remembering the look on her face the morning she came into Lizann Falvey's quarters and found him there. She had seen the gun, and she had seen Lizann's hands on his shoulders.

He felt someone behind him and as he turned, Karla said, "Would you like coffee?"

"Fine . . . I was just thinking about you."

"I'll bring you a cup." She started to turn away.

"Karla—" His hand touched her arm, but came away as she looked up at him again. "We never have much time to talk, do we?"

"I guess not."

"We ought to have about a week with nothing else to do but talk, to get caught up with each other." He paused. "Karla . . . I'm grateful for what you've done. I've thought about it and thought about it, but I don't know how to say it."

"Is that why you escaped, to come thank us?"

Bowen frowned. "I tried to explain that to your father." He spoke earnestly, keeping his voice low. "You can feel you've done right, but when you explain it, it doesn't sound like good sense."

Karla's eyes raised to his. "I'm sorry. I shouldn't have said that. You had no reason to believe a new trial would come through."

"I was hopeful. But then this chance came along."

"If only I could have gotten to you before—"

"Well, it's done now."

"The morning you were with Lizann"—Karla's eyes moved to the window—"I wanted to tell you about it then. But you were there and then gone. I asked Lizann to tell you we'd found out something and not to use the gun." She paused. "No . . . I even told her Mr. Martz had filed a motion for a new trial!"

Bowen shook his head. "She didn't tell me anything about it. Listen . . . that's something else. She had good reason not to tell me." He glanced toward Falvey at the bar and brought Karla closer to him. "I've got something on my mind and I don't know what to do about it. Lizann didn't just give me that gun for my sake." He glanced toward the bar again, then back to Karla. "She wanted me to use it on Willis."

Karla's lips parted. But for a moment she stared, saying nothing. "You're sure?"

"She said I could do anything I wanted with it—if I used it on Willis first."

"It's hard to believe a woman—"

"Listen, I was standing right in front of her and I had trouble believing it."

"But you took the gun," Karla said.

"Of course I took it. I wanted to get *out*. I would have promised to shoot President Cleveland if she'd asked me. That kind of promise doesn't mean anything."

Karla said, "Have you told Willis?"

"No. That's what's bothering me. But he saw me come in here with the gun and he even guessed how I got it."

"Maybe he thinks there's something between you and Lizann."

"I don't know. Maybe he does."

"Is there?" Karla asked hesitatingly.

"Because we were standing so close that time?"

"That would seem to suggest—"

"Karla, she wasn't taking any chances. If I didn't feel sorry for her enough to do it, then maybe she could make me like her enough to."

"I wasn't going to ask you that," Karla said. "It just came out."

He watched her eyes and the clean line of her nose and her mouth. "It's something, isn't it? We've only talked together twice before this."

Karla nodded looking up at him and was silent for a moment. "What are you going to do?"

"Now?"

She smiled. "What would you do after. If—"

"After, I was planning to visit Willcox. I've got a friend there in the mining business. He doesn't mine there, but that's where his office is and where he ships out of. He's been after me to join him for a long time. In fact, I was on my way there when I met Earl."

"That's where my mother is," Karla said. "My sisters are in school there."

"You've got sisters?"

"Two younger ones."

"I could look them up."

"It isn't far. I go down every once in a while."

"We could sure get to know each other, couldn't we?"

"But," Karla said, "it seems a long way off."

"Now we're back," Bowen said.

Karla smiled faintly. "I'm glad we did that." She paused. "Are you going to tell Willis?"

"I don't want to. Even if he suspects her, *knowing* it is something else."

"Maybe she's sorry now."

"Maybe she is. I don't know."

"You'd think they would have parted before this."

"Renda wouldn't let them."

"What if Willis still likes her?" Karla said.

"That'd be something."

"Corey...don't tell him. If he already suspects her, he must be on his guard—"

"Or else he doesn't care."

"At least wait and see how this comes out. If there's a hearing, then you know she'll take the opportunity to leave him."

"But if Renda wins there's won't be a hearing and everybody'll be right back where they started."

"Don't let him win," Karla said earnestly.

"Karla, I keep going over it and going over it—I can't just use a gun on him. If I killed him I'd be back in jail—or worse—and Willis wouldn't have to say a word. If we hold Renda and force a hearing, we can't prove anything unless Willis testifies."

"But Lizann would," Karla said.

"You can't count on her. She might keep still, afraid the plan to kill Willis would come out. Or she might just run off."

Karla nodded. "So Willis is the only hope."

"And he knows he'll go to jail if he speaks up."

"Corey...what will you do when he comes?"

"I wish I knew."

There was silence before Karla said, "He doesn't know Willis is here. Every other time Willis has gone to Fuegos. Sometimes he stops for a drink on the way. But this time he stayed...and Renda couldn't know that."

"Your father mentioned it. I don't know how it can help us—" Bowen stopped. "Unless—"

"Unless," Karla said eagerly, "you can make him tell what he did to Lizann *in front of Willis!* He won't believe it from us—"

"He doesn't want to believe it," Bowen said.

"But he'd have to believe Renda. And in front of all of us he'd have to do something—that's what I mean!"

"If I was Willis I wouldn't much care."

"But you're not Willis! He said he didn't *believe* us...not he didn't *care*. That's why I'd be willing to bet anything he still likes her."

"You sure have a feeling about people."

"I was right about you, wasn't I?"

"You and that Mimbre would get along fine."

Karla frowned, but she ignored this and said, "Is it worth a try or isn't it?"

"I suppose it is," Bowen said slowly. Then, "Tell your father to keep Willis out of sight when Frank comes, but close enough to hear." Bowen shook his head. "I don't even know what I'm going to say. Your father gave me an envelope to pass off as the one Frank's looking for, but I don't know how I'd work that. I've got all kinds of tricks and I don't know how I'm going to spring any of them."

"You could pretend to make a deal with him," Karla said eagerly. "Renda gets the letter if he lets you go. At least you'd have a chance of getting away from here."

Bowen shrugged. "I don't know."

Karla smiled up at him. "You'll think of something." Turning away she said, "I'll bring your coffee now."

But within thirty seconds the coffee was forgotten and there was no time to think of what he would say. As Bowen looked out across the yard again, he saw Frank Renda ride out of the willows.

SEVENTEEN

BOWEN drew the Colt from his belt, pressing himself against the wall next to the window. He looked across the room seeing Karla and her father in the kitchen, then waited until Demery turned from her and started into the front room.

"He's here," Bowen said. He nodded toward Falvey, saw Falvey turn from the bar as Demery started for him, then Bowen's gaze returned to the window.

Renda came at a walk, moving easily with the motion of the big chestnut. The shotgun was across his lap and his eyes remained on the adobe as he approached.

Behind him, Bowen heard Falvey's voice. A protest. Then steps going into the kitchen. Bowen moved three steps along the wall to the next window as Renda drew closer. He watched Renda come to a stop five or six yards out from the door. Now he'll call, Bowen thought.

But there was no call. Renda waited, apparently listening, then reined the chestnut to the left and started along the front of the open shed.

Bowen pressed close to the window, then came away from it suddenly. He saw Karla in the kitchen, doorway, motioned to her and moved quietly to meet her. "He's going around back. Get Willis's horse out of sight—quick!"

He stepped to the window again, saw Renda nearing the end of the shed, made sure he was turning the corner, then hurried to the kitchen. Karla was already outside. Demery, standing behind Falvey who was seated at the table, raised his eyes inquiringly.

"He's coming around," Bowen said.

"What's Karla doing?"

"She's all right."

Bowen moved to the wooden sink and pressed against the drainboard to look out the window. He saw Karla holding the dun close to the bit, her left hand on its nose, leading it along the stable shed that extended out from the house and almost to the corral. She reached the end of the

154

shed and rounded it a moment before Renda came into the yard.

As Renda looked toward the house, Bowen stepped away from the window. Then, hearing the horse's hoofs again, he moved along the wall to the door and looked out, edging past the side frame.

The chestnut was broadside to him, facing the shed, ten yards out and directly in line with the door. Renda sat motionless, half turned from Bowen and staring off toward the end of the shed. His right hand was on the shotgun and he seemed to be listening.

He'd have to come around to use it, Bowen thought. Or turn it over and shoot left-handed.

Bowen eased open the screen door and stepped outside. Instantly the sunlight struck him and he wanted to pull his hat brim closer to his eyes, but he hesitated with the thought of his hand momentarily in front of his face. Without thinking the word fear he realized it was fear that made him hesitate, and now, deliberately, he pulled the straw brim straight over his eyes, telling himself to relax and get hold of himself, before he brought up the Colt, cocking it as he did.

"Frank—"

Renda's body twisted in the saddle. Seeing Bowen, his face showed surprise, but it was momentary and only in his eyes. He stared at Bowen intently, saying nothing, and Bowen could almost read what was passing through his mind.

"Don't even think about it," Bowen warned. "You wouldn't get it halfway around."

Renda seemed to relax. "You'll never learn, will you? Put the gun down and tell Earl to come out."

"Earl's not in this."

"He's already gone?"

Bowen shook his head. "But he's out of it. This is just between you and me."

"Listen, you're in enough trouble. Put the gun down." Renda waited. The Colt remained leveled at him. "Corey, you're going to strain yourself standing like that." Renda's left heel nudged the chestnut and its forelegs side-stepped toward the porch.

"Hold it!"

Renda was almost facing Bowen now. He smiled, saying, "You got poor nerves, Corey."

"Let the shotgun drop and they'll be all right."

"What if it went off?"

"So will this if it does."

"You won't get more than a mile," Renda said. "You know that. The Mimbres'll be all over you."

"Are you sure?"

Renda shrugged. "You ought to know it better than I do."

"Let go of the shotgun, Frank."

"If I don't what'll you do, shoot me?"

"I might have to."

"Use your head. You got, what—six years to serve. You'd trade that for a rope?"

Bowen hesitated. Something was forming in his mind, but he was not yet sure if it could be developed. He said then, "What would you trade to stay alive?"

"I don't see where I have to trade anything."

Now, Bowen thought. "What about the letter you came for?"

Renda grinned. "Little Karla's been telling you things."

"Look at it this way," Bowen said. "Would you give your life to try to get the letter?"

For a moment Renda was silent and he nodded thoughtfully. "I've been figuring you all wrong, haven't I?"

"You see what it comes to?" Bowen said carefully.

Renda shrugged. "But I'm not even sure Karla's got the letter."

"You wouldn't be here if you weren't."

"The thing is," Renda said slowly. "I don't see you come out smelling any better than you went in. What do you get out of it?"

"I get what you trade for the letter."

"So we're making a deal." Renda grinned. "I must be a little slow this morning."

Bowen nodded. "But now everything's clear."

"Where's the letter now?"

Bowen's hand touched his pocket. "Right here."

"Let's see it."

Bowen's eyes remained on Renda as his hand went to his pocket and brought out the envelope Demery had given him. He glanced at it and saw it was addressed to Demery.

"Frank, it says: to the District Supervisor, Bureau of"—Bowen looked up. "I can't read all of Lizann's writing." Then, glancing at the envelope again, "Department of the Interior, Prescott, Arizona Territory . . . That mean anything to you?"

"I don't know if it does," Renda answered. "I haven't read it. Have you?"

"I don't have to—I've been living with you."

Renda leaned forward. "Let's see it."

"Not till we talk about a swap."

Renda was silent. "How about this?" he said then. "You give me the letter and I give you a ten-minute start. Take a horse and keep your gun."

Bowen smiled faintly. "You believe in starting low."

"You want a half hour?"

Get somewhere, Bowen thought, but said, still not sure where this would lead. "What about the Mimbres?"

"That's your problem"

Bowen shook his head. "They're yours now."

"All right . . . I'll call them off."

"How?"

"Ride ahead—tell them to let you through."

"Even if I trusted you, I wouldn't go for that."

"You're hard to please." Renda paused, then said, "Here's another way. You come back to the camp and we'll fix it for you to slip out at night. You'd have about a six-hour start."

"You're bidding low again," Bowen said. "The more I think about it, the more it looks like I'm only safe if I stay close to you. Even if I did get away I'd be hiding out the rest of my life . . . while you're making all that money on the road."

He spoke slowly, thinking ahead of what he was saying and suddenly, there it was: a way to bring Falvey into it. A natural, part-of-the-conversation way that would arouse neither Renda's suspicion nor Falvey's—if he was listening. And Bowen thought, wanting to look around at the adobe but making himself keep his eyes on Renda: Willis, be listening!

He said then, "What I need, Frank, is a deal something like Willis Falvey's. We'd each have something on the other, and we'd get along fine."

Renda studied Bowen in silence.

157

"Fix me a deal like that, Frank. I get so much of your profits for not mailing the letter."

"Somebody's been talking to you," Renda said quietly.

"Maybe it was Willis," Bowen said. "Maybe he's getting tired."

"Willis knows better."

"Maybe he's so tired he's going to stand up to you."

"Where would he get the nerve?"

"He's got it, Frank. He's had enough all along to think of his wife first . . . to stay out of jail for her sake."

"You think so, huh?"

"He made a mistake getting tied to you, but once he was in, it took nerve to keep going. The wrong kind of nerve, but at least you know he's got it." Bowen paused, thinking: You hear that, Willis? "Sometimes a man will put up with anything for his wife. That's where you misjudged him."

Renda said, "You don't know as much about him as I thought."

"But now," Bowen went on, "he's tired of it. He's starting to think it would be worth going to jail for a year or two just to get it off his mind. He realizes now his wife would respect him more if he did. After that he'd be a free agent and all the Frank Rendas in the world could go to hell."

"He knows he'd get more than a jail sentence," Renda said. "I'd bust his head for him."

"Would you?" Bowen paused. He said then, slowly, clearly, "Is that what you did to Lizann?"

Renda stared at him. "Karla didn't forget anything, did she?"

"She'll probably never forget it," Bowen said, "seeing a woman beat up. Did you have a hard time?"

"She got what she asked for."

"Frank, you're a real fighter, aren't you?" A sound came from the kitchen. Bowen heard it close behind him, but he was not sure what it was. "You fight women . . . and men with their hands tied behind them."

Renda's intent expression did not change. "You're getting off the subject, aren't you?"

"We've got time," Bowen said easily. He was thinking, hurriedly: Keep him on it! "Frank, what's it like to hit a woman?"

"You're asking a lot of questions," Renda said.

"Do you let her fight back?"

This time Renda did not answer.

"Or do you get her against the wall and just keep swinging at her?"

"You're leading up to something," Renda said cautiously.

"Frank, what's Willis going to do when he finds out?"

"He'll figure he's lucky it didn't happen to him."

"You know what I'd do if I were Willis?" Bowen paused. "I'd take a pick handle to you."

"You would, huh?"

Bowen nodded. "I'd crack you ten for every one time you hit her."

Then, close behind him, not expecting it, the screen door swung open. As he heard it, Bowen moved aside, almost glancing back, but at the same moment, seeing the look of shocked surprise come over Renda's face, he knew it was Willis Falvey, just as he knew, suddenly feeling more sure of himself, that Falvey had been listening all the time. Still watching Renda, he thought: If he moves hit him in the leg. He glanced quickly to the side then. Falvey was staring up at Renda. Lizann's .25-caliber Colt in his hand.

"Frank . . . you put your filthy hands on my wife?"

Renda shifted his weight in the saddle. "Willis, I didn't know you were here."

"Answer me!"

"Listen, Willis. I'm sorry that had to happen. It was Lizann's own fault. She didn't have to get hit but she wouldn't tell me—" He stopped. "Willis, she was planning to leave you. You realize that?"

"Frank," Falvey said tonelessly. "When you're through talking I'm going to kill you."

"Use your head! She's going to leave you anyway. She don't care a damn about you."

Bowen glanced at Falvey. "Killing him isn't the way. *Testify* against him in court. He didn't just beat up your wife—men died in that place because of him, men like Chick Miller. You'll see him dead—but let a jury take care of it!"

"I'll testify," Falvey said. "But Frank won't be there to hear it."

"So you shoot him and they hang you. You think it's worth it?"

"I'd as soon that happen as go to prison," Falvey answered. "You're wasting your breath."

Renda moved uneasily in the saddle, his hands gripping the shotgun. "Willis—listen to him—he's talking sense!"

Falvey stared, "Are you through?"

"Man, stop and think for a minute!"

"You're through," Falvey murmured.

He brought up the revolver, leveling it at Renda's chest, thumbing back the hammer. It was in his mind to kill Renda and there was no persuading him otherwise—but as he pulled the trigger, Bowen slammed against him. The revolver fired wide as both of them went down, and with the report Renda was reining hard to the right, kicking the chestnut; he fired from his lap as the big mare wheeled, but the shot was hurried and ripped high through the screen door.

Falvey was up as the mare broke into a gallop angling to the left of the corral. He fired once, then again. Bowen was on one knee as he saw Renda twist in the saddle and point the shotgun back with one hand.

"Go down!"

But he called too late. Renda's second barrel exploded. He saw Falvey spin sideways as the buckshot hailed against the adobe, chipping a powdery cloud, and Falvey went down, dropping the revolver and suddenly clutching his left hip.

Then Demery was outside, lifting Falvey, holding open the shot-out screen door with his foot and dragging Falvey into the kitchen. He snapped at Bowen, glancing off at Renda, "Get him—what's the matter with you!"

"Watch," Bowen said, coming to his feet. His eyes were narrowed, his gaze following Renda as he reached the far side of the corral and rode on toward the pine-covered slope beyond.

Demery came out again. "You let him get away!"

"Watch," Bowen said again. And as their eyes followed the chestnut moving across the meadow, streaking for the dark expanse of trees, they saw it veer sharply to the right. A single file of riders had suddenly appeared, coming down out of the trees.

Renda circled, waving his shotgun in the air and the riders, the Mimbres, came after him. As he continued the wide circle, gradually coming back to the yard, another file of Mimbres rode out of the trees approximately two hundred yards farther to the right, joining the first group now and spreading out behind Renda who glanced back at them, waving them on with the shotgun, then began to rein in as he neared the corral again.

"They're backing him!" Demery hissed.

"Wait and see," Bowen said, not taking his eyes from Renda. Then asked, "Where's Karla?"

"Inside," Demery murmured. "Looking after Willis. She circled around and came in the front. Stood there biting her nails through the whole thing...like to got hit when Frank ripped up the door."

"What about Willis?"

"His side's scraped is all."

"Was he listening...before?"

"Hanging on every word you said...like courage being poured into him." Demery watched Renda wave the Mimbres past him. "Listen, you can't just stand there!"

Bowen said nothing, watching four of the Mimbres circle the corral to come in on the left side. The others—he counted six—Salvaje one of them, rode past Renda. They entered the yard, moving past the corral and spread out in an uneven line as they came to a halt.

Now, Bowen thought; and walked out toward them. He was halfway across the yard when Renda came through the line of Mimbres and reined in a few yards in front of them. Bowen continued toward him until less than fifteen feet separated them.

"That's far enough," Renda called. "Now drop the shooter."

Bowen held the Colt at his side, pointed at the ground. "It won't do you any good."

"Drop it!"

Bowen let it fall from his fingers.

"Now kick it out of the way."

With the side of his foot, Bowen pushed the Colt away from him.

"The deal's off." Renda grinned. He was relaxed and confident now and looked at Bowen with open amusement. "Give me the letter."

"It wouldn't do you any good even if there was one," Bowen said. "Since Willis is going to speak up against you."

Renda's eyes narrowed. "He's still alive?"

"You just scraped his hip."

"Well, I'll have a talk with Willis," Renda said easily.

161

"I've found Willis an agreeable boy if you talk to him right."
His tone changed as he snapped. "Now give me the letter!"

Bowen brought the folded envelope from his pocket. He
moved close to the chestnut's right shoulder, handed the
envelope to Renda and stepped back again.

Renda glanced at it, saw Demery's address and looked
at Bowen again. "You just pulled twenty more days in the
punishment cell."

Bowen said nothing.

Renda's gaze raised to the adobe. Demery was still at
the door. "John, where's that letter your girl brought?"

Demery shook his head holding his palms up.

"I'm warning you, John—"

"He doesn't have it," Bowen said. "Nobody does."

"I can burn down the house if that's what he wants."

"There never was a letter, Frank. Lizann made it up to
get rid of you. But you happened to see Karla and you
believed her."

"If there's no letter," Renda said, "then why'd you try to
make a deal? You think I'd have let you go without even
looking at it?"

"That was leading up to something else," Bowen said. "I
wasn't going anywhere."

"You sure as hell weren't."

"I didn't know how I was going to use the letter at first,"
Bowen said. "I just had it as an extra card. Then, somewhere along the line, it steered us to Willis."

"I'm not going to ask you again."

"Check with your men in the canyon then! They saw
Karla go by *after* you left for the camp. Karla didn't even
drop off the mail she had, much less pick any up."

Renda looked past Bowen toward the adobe. "We'll see."

Bowen shook his head. "You're not going in there."

"Who's going to stop me?"

"Frank, you've got a surprise coming."

"I'm getting awful sick of you," Renda said slowly.

"But you're not going in," Bowen said. "Not with Willis
there."

For a moment Renda was silent. "Corey...I think I've
had just about all I can take of you." His right hand went
into his coat pocket and brought out a shell for the shotgun. He broke open the gun, still watching Bowen, and
carefully inserted the shell into the right chamber.

"What you're going to do," Renda said, taking his time and seeming to enjoy what he was saying, "is make a run for it. But if you move before I give the word, these bucks will blow you apart."

Bowen watched Renda's hand move to the pocket. The hand raised then and pointed off to the far side of the corral.

"That's the way you go," Renda said. "With a ten-count start. If you can run like hell, maybe you'll almost reach the trees."

"What about the witnesses?" Bowen said. He watched Renda's hand drop to his thigh.

"Who's going to say you didn't try to run?" Renda answered. His hand moved to the pocket and brought out a shell. He glanced down at the open shotgun and started inserting the shell into the left chamber.

It was the moment Bowen was waiting for. He lunged at Renda, reaching up for him.

The shotgun snapped closed and exploded over Bowen's shoulder as he dragged Renda from the saddle, one hand on the barrel, the other gripping Renda's sleeve, twisting then, throwing his shoulder into Renda's stomach as they both went to the ground.

Renda rolled free. He started to rise, coming to one knee, swinging the shotgun in line, but he was a moment too late and as he pulled the trigger the barrel rose suddenly and fired into the air. Bowen's left hand twisted the barrel, Renda cried out, his finger caught in the trigger guard, and as he released the shotgun, Bowen's right hand slammed against the side of his face.

Renda went down, rolled again and shielded his face with his arms as he came to his knees. Then, seeing Bowen standing, holding the shotgun, not coming for him, his gaze swung to the Mimbres, to Salvaje.

"Bust him!"

Salvaje made no move.

"You hear me!" Renda screamed. "Bust him!"

Salvaje held his Springfield straight up, the stock resting on his thigh. His eyes were on Renda, but he did not move.

Renda hesitated, his chest rising and falling. His gaze moved along the line of Mimbres, over the cloth headbands and the stone-silent stares, the slanting cartridge bandoleers and the Springfields leveled across the pommels of their saddles. All of them were watching him and only Salvaje's carbine pointed into the air.

"You hear me!" Renda screamed again. "Cut him down! Now!"

"They hear you," Bowen said.

Renda's eyes did not leave Salvaje. "What's the matter with you? I said *shoot* him!"

Then silence, and Bowen said. "There's your surprise, Frank." He watched Renda turn slowly to face him. "You were in such a rush to get back," Bowen went on, "you didn't find out if you were leading or being chased."

For a long moment Renda said nothing. "What did you tell them?" he asked finally.

"What difference does it make. You don't have your guns, you don't have any men and Willis is against you . . . Why don't you quit now?"

Renda's eyes stared from the shadow of his hatbrim, not moving from Bowen. His mustache masked the grim line of his mouth and his jaw was clenched tightly. He stared at Bowen, silent with his thoughts, and the hate came slowly into his eyes. Finally, then, he started toward Bowen, walking slowly, his head slightly down, but his eyes raised and not wavering as he came on.

Bowen held the shotgun in his right hand, the barrel pointed at the ground. "Frank, my hands aren't tied this time."

Renda came on.

"And I'm not Lizann," Bowen said.

Another two steps . . . three . . . on the next one, Renda hesitated, then rushed at Bowen. At the same moment, Bowen swung the shotgun, letting it go at Renda's legs. Renda tried to dodge, bringing himself up, but the barrel cracked across his ankles and he stumbled forward.

Bowen had half turned as he threw the gun; now his body swung back and his left hand hammered against Renda's face. Renda tried to cover, bringing up his arms, but Bowen's right slammed through his guard; he tried to fight back, swinging blindly, viciously, but Bowen's right hand jabbed again and again and he was forced to cover his face. As he did, Bowen side-stepped and came in with a wide swinging left that opened Renda's guard and jolted him back off balance. Bowen followed, shifting his feet, hammering in with his right hand, and as Renda staggered back, Bowen kept with him, hooking in one hand then the other, slashing Renda across the mouth and eyes, putting almost his full weight behind each blow, until Renda dropped. He tried to rise, then fell heavily on his back. His arms were outstretched now and he didn't move.

Bowen's arms hung at his sides. The muscles in them ached and he opened and closed his hands painfully. He felt exhaustion and relief, looking down at Renda, thinking now of all that had happened over the past hour, seeing Karla and Falvey and Renda and the Mimbreños, briefly remembering words, pieces of conversations, but not seeing or thinking these things in proper order and he wasn't sure if all of it had actually happened.

He heard footsteps in the yard, someone coming out from the house, but he turned to the Mimbres first and walked toward them, to Salvaje who had dismounted.

"If we were to talk for a few days," Bowen said to him, "with tulapai between us, maybe I could tell you how I feel."

"Come to San Carlos," the Mimbreño said.

"They won't send you back," Bowen said. "Whoever comes out to take Renda's place will still want trackers."

The broad brim of Salvaje's hat moved slightly as he shook his head. "We go home. This is not like other times. I think Victorio would laugh." The Mimbre watched Bowen closely. "Do you understand that?"

Bowen's head nodded slowly. "Yes ... I think I do."

Salvaje's eyes went to Renda. "He will be in the punishment cell until they come for him."

Demery approached. He was smiling, looking from Renda, who was still on the ground, to Bowen. "He didn't even put a hand on you!"

"Not this time," Bowen said.

"About Falvey," Demery said. "There wasn't time to tell you before ... That was something to see. Soon as you and Frank started talking about him he got up and moved closer to the window, and after a minute he didn't seem drunk anymore, or even afraid. He just stood staring at the wall ... I never felt so sorry for a man in all my life. There you were handing him a chance to prove himself a man and you could see him trying his damndest to work up enough courage to take it." Demery shook his head.

"That's something I'll never forget." He looked toward Renda again. "And Frank not even knowing what was happening."

"I'm not sure I knew either." Bowen said. "Or know yet." He saw Karla and moved past Demery to meet her. "Is Willis all right?"

Karla smiled. "He's in bed with your friend. Propped up with a drink next to him and pen and paper on his lap. He asked for it. He said if he didn't do another thing, he was going to get it off his chest right now...Come see." She took his hand and as they walked off toward the house, she asked, "But what about Lizann?"

Lizann, Bowen thought wearily. You forgot Lizann. "I don't know. Maybe she's gone by now. If she is, Willis is better off without her. But maybe she's learned her lesson ...And a few more maybes for good measure."

"You're tired," Karla said quietly.

All that he had been thinking and trying to remember was still in his mind; though less vividly now and as he walked toward the adobe, Karla close at his side and the awareness of her coming over him more strongly, more relaxingly, the pieces of conversation and the images began to dissolve: the Mimbres, Willis Falvey, the road, even Frank Renda—there was no reason to think about them now. Somehow it had happened and somehow it was over.

Only Karla remained.

ABOUT THE AUTHOR

ELMORE LEONARD has written over fifteen novels and numerous short stories, several of which have been turned into successful films including *3:10 to Yuma* and *Valdez Is Coming*. He has also written the screenplays for such films as *Joe Kidd,* starring Clint Eastwood, and *Mr. Majestyk,* starring Charles Bronson. His novel, *Hombre,* was chosen as one of the twenty-five best Western novels ever written by the Western Writers of America. *The Switch,* published by Bantam, was nominated by the Mystery Writers of America for the Edgar Allan Poe Award for the best paperback of 1978.

BANTAM
SHOP-AT-HOME
C·A·T·A·L·O·G

Special Offer
Buy a Bantam Book
for only 50¢.

Now you can have Bantam's catalog filled with hundreds of titles plus take advantage of our unique and exciting bonus book offer. A special offer which gives you the opportunity to purchase a Bantam book for only 50¢. Here's how!

By ordering any five books at the regular price per order, you can also choose any other single book listed (up to a $4.95 value) for just 50¢. Some restrictions do apply, but for further details why not send for Bantam's catalog of titles today!

Just send us your name and address and we will send you a catalog!